UNBAKED CROAKIES

SAM CHEEVER

ELECTRIC PROSE PUBLICATIONS

How in the name of the goddess's favorite sports bra am I going to do this Magical Librarian job? I have no idea what I'm doing. And the woman who's supposed to be training me is...well, let's just say she's distracted and leave it at that. I guess I'll bumble through. It's become something of a trademark move for me.

My name is Naida Griffith and I'm a sorceress. I actually found that out not too long ago. I've lived with an undefined something burning in my belly for a while, feeling as if something wasn't quite right under my skin. Then, on my eighteenth birthday I started getting headaches. Bad ones. And random stuff started following me around.

Recently I was approached by a group called the Société of Dire Magic to become Keeper of the Artifacts. A magical librarian. Given that magical artifacts have taken to following me around, I decided I might have an aptitude for the job. So I said yes.

But in the first few days, I've been flogged by flip flops, bludgeoned by gnomes, and discovered a corpse in a suitcase. Then there's the woman who's supposed to be training me. She's...interesting.

Will I survive the training long enough to get the job as artifact librarian? You might as well ask me if a caterpillar gets manis or pedis. Who knows? But I know one thing for sure. This gig is hard.

I'm going to do my best to succeed. Or die trying.

OY, PUDSY. HOW'S THINGS?

I stood on the street outside the bookstore, frowning up at the ugly wood sign with the picture of a spotted frog on it. The yellowed white paint was chipped and scarred, and there was a black blotch near the frog's mouth that looked like a fly.

I kept expecting the frog's tongue to snake out and snap it up.

It was an ugly sign. World-class ugly. But it was oddly suited given the store's strange name.

Croakies.

I mean. What kind of name was that for a bookstore?

Soft footsteps came up behind me and I resisted turning.

"Are you ready?"

At just under six feet, the man was only a few

inches taller than I was. I guessed he was about middle age. For a sorcerer that would put him in his eighties or nineties. He had piercing blue eyes that were a little darker than mine and longish, curly brown hair. He also had a truly forgettable face. I mean that literally. From one moment to the next I would often forget what the man looked like. In fact, the few times I'd seen him, I'd only been able to identify him because of the sorcerer's garb he wore.

The thought made me frown.

I always remembered the piercing blue gaze. And the hair. But that was all that stuck in my mind.

I knew him only as Agent A.P. from the Société of Dire Magic. A formidable group whose moniker seemed to strike fear into the hearts of everyone I spoke to about them. Supernormals, at least. Since I'd been raised by a non-magical grandma, I didn't really know that many supernormals. But the few I'd met since A.P. had knocked on my door a couple of weeks earlier, had seemed more than half afraid of him.

I had no idea what it was that scared them about the man. He seemed harmless enough to me.

I turned to look at the agent. He was less intimidating in his street clothes than he'd been in his robes. I'd only met him a handful of times. But each time we'd met previously, he'd looked just like a fairytale sorcerer in his long purple and black robes. All that had been missing was the pointy hat.

And the wand.

When I'd jokingly asked him where those two items were, he'd very earnestly explained that they were only for special ceremonies.

I hadn't known him long enough to recognize if he was joking.

I chose to believe he was.

Otherwise, it would just be too weird.

But back to his question. *Was I ready?*

Taking a deep, bracing breath, I nodded. I was as ready as I was ever going to be. With a feeling that my life was about to change in ways I couldn't imagine and might not like, I reached for the door to Croakies and opened it.

A mangy black cat galloped toward the door as it opened, yowling as if he were being chased by an army of slavering canines. The feline's headlong flight was accompanied by a prolonged shriek.

"Banshee Botox!" a woman caterwauled from deep inside the store. "Close the door! Don't let him out."

I quickly slammed the door behind me, cutting the agent behind me off in mid-stride.

A.P. yelped in pain from the wrong side of the entrance.

A woman came scurrying out of the stacks, rushing over to grab the cat, who was almost as big as a full-sized dachshund and sported only one and a half ears.

The feline's longish black fur was matted and sparse in spots, making him look like he'd spent the better part his life on the streets. White fur speckled the big cat's cheeks and chin, marking him as a feline of the older variety. His large, expressive eyes were a silvery-green and probably the most attractive thing about him.

Which wasn't saying much.

"Fenwald, you naughty boy," the woman said, her accent strident and British. "You're getting that bath whether you want it or not."

She looked at me through a pair of large tortoise-shell glasses, shoving them up a pug nose and peering at me as if I were a particularly nasty bug. "What is it, then? Do ya need a book?"

The door behind me opened, and A.P. came inside the store, rubbing his decidedly red nose. He glared at the woman behind the square glasses. "Alice. That cat is a menace."

I expected her to buckle under his severe disappointment. Instead, she grinned.

"Oy, Pudsy. How's things? You're looking a bit pinkish about the old snout there, eh?" Her laughter was a series of odd snorts that vibrated the glasses down her nose. She reached up and poked them back into place with a bandaged finger covered in black ink. "Ah," she said, her smallish brown eyes rolling back to me. "So, this is my new apprentice, then?" She looked me over with a critical eye. "She'll do." The woman offered me a work-roughened hand. "I'm Alice, Keeper of the Artifacts. You're Naida?"

I nodded, struck dumb by the reality in front of me. In my mind, I'd pictured a tall, powerful woman with a calm, no-nonsense manner as KoA, which is what the magical universe called Keepers of the Artifacts. My imagination might have even given her a long staff that shot electricity from the tip. Alice didn't fit that image in any respect.

Jerking her head toward the side, Alice said. "Come on, then. I'll make us a spot of tea." She carried the big cat with her as she slouched toward a nook across from the sales counter. The space sported a miniature stove, a tiny sink, and a short counter, which was covered in tea-making things and had a small refrigerator tucked beneath it. The oven door was open, and a comfortable warmth oozed from its interior. The cat immediately sprawled in front of it and began to bathe, clearly enjoying the heat.

With a jolt, I realized Alice was using the ancient appliance to warm the bookstore. "Is the heater broken?" I asked, pulling my coat closer as I shivered. I wasn't looking forward to spending a winter shivering and sniffling day and night.

Alice flipped a dismissive hand. "It's just having a fit. It'll be right as rain in no time."

I sent A.P. a worried glance, and he shook his

head. "You need to get that fixed, Alice," he told the woman. "It was part of your apprenticeship agreement with the Société."

She ignored him completely, motioning negligently toward the small, three-person table in the center of the open space at the front of the store. A high, narrow window above the tea nook showed the clear blue of an early-January sky. The bright sunshine painted a golden ribbon across the bookstore's ratty carpet and bathed the round table in warmth. "Have a seat, Naida." She glanced at A.P. "You too, Pudsy. I'll have tea ready in two shakes."

I looked at A.P. and smiled, mouthing, "Pudsy?"

He shook his head dismissively.

While the tea steeped, Alice pulled the oven door wide. Grabbing a dingy towel that was appliqued with a large black cat which looked nothing like Fenwald, she tugged a flat pan from the oven's interior. She carefully extracted three pale, oblong biscuits from the pan, arranging them like spokes on a wheel in the center of a chipped white plate and sliding the rest back inside the oven.

Alice placed the snack on the table between us. "Scones. My specialty."

Having missed breakfast that morning, I smiled in anticipation. "Thank you. They smell delicious."

Alice gave me a pleased smile and returned to her tea prep.

Fenwald wandered over and sat down a few feet

away from the table, staring at me through an unfathomable green gaze.

I reached for a scone, eyeing the dark spots marking its golden surface and wondering what they were. I hoped they weren't raisins. *Maybe blueberries?* I thought, hopefully.

A.P. reached out and touched my hand with a finger, shaking his head and frowning as I lifted it toward my mouth.

Grinning, I took a bite.

"Ow!" I said before I could stop myself.

A.P. sat back and shook his head.

"Watch out, sweetums. They're hot."

I pulled the scone from my mouth and looked at the shallow dent my teeth had made in it. Feeling my front teeth to make sure they were still intact, I arched my brows at A.P.

He chuckled soundlessly. Reaching for another scone, he held it above the table for a moment, glancing over at Alice, he asked, "Is that a new thriller section, Alice?"

The Keeper lifted her head and looked into the bookstore. "Yes. Blimey, you do have a keen eye. I moved them from the back because I've seen new interest in thrillers of late." Alice wandered over to the books in question and ran her hand lovingly over their perfectly arranged spines.

While she was distracted. The Société agent slammed his scone against the edge of the table, coughing loudly to cover the noise, and broke a large chunk off the end of it. He threw the piece to Fenwald. It hit the carpet with the weight of a large marble and skittered to a spot a few inches from the cat.

Fenwald eyed the heavy offering and then lifted a derisive gaze to A.P., as if to say, *I'm not eating that.* Not wasting any time considering the offering, the big cat reached out with a large paw and whacked it away.

We watched it skitter beneath the cabinet where Alice kept her assortment of teas, out of sight.

I wondered how many other bits of bad baking the cat had "stored" beneath the cabinet. Then I decided I probably didn't want to know.

"I find I'm growing fond of the genre," Alice said, oblivious as she returned to her tea-making. She glanced over her shoulder at me. "How about you, Naida? What's your favorite genre?"

I flushed in embarrassment, not wanting to tell her in front of A.P. "Um, paranormal." It wasn't a lie...exactly...I did like some paranormal along with my romance.

Alice's grin widened. "A fine choice. I have a large selection in the store. Help yourself if you'd like. Just be sure to put a couple of dollars in the till for the rent."

My eyes went wide. "Rent?" There'd been no mention of rent. I'd thought I was going to be working off my room and board. It was an old-fashioned arrangement but a necessity. When my grandma had died a few months previous, she'd left me with a tiny house filled with ratty furnishings and a lot of debt that pretty much wiped out whatever I would earn from the sale of the house.

I had no money and no family that I knew of. If Agent A.P. hadn't come to me and told me there was an apprenticeship open for an artifact librarian, I'd have been in sad shape.

For once in my life, it had seemed like the winds of fate had blown in my favor. Though the Société agent had been vague about how he'd found me, murmuring something about being a friend of my grandma's.

I highly doubted that.

"Yes," said Alice. "I rent books for avid readers who don't have the space to store them all."

I nodded in understanding. "That makes sense."

She placed cups of tea in front of us and then pulled a third chair from the corner. Dropping into it with a sigh, Alice Parker fixed a speculative look on me. Then, lifting her teacup to her mouth, she said, "So, Naida Griffith, tell me why I should hire you as an apprentice for Keeper of the Artifacts?"

My mind went blank. I glanced toward A.P., but he wasn't paying attention to us. He'd pulled out his cell phone and seemed to be checking his emails.

I was on my own.

"Um..." I said stupidly. Stalling for time, I tucked a long strand of my curly brown hair behind one ear. Digging deep, I discarded options as quickly as they occurred to me. I couldn't tell her it was because I'd just turned twenty-two and needed a job. From what A.P. had told me, Keepers were born to wrangle artifacts. It wasn't a career choice. It was their legacy. I didn't want Alice to know I wasn't really suited for the job. She'd find out soon enough.

After a moment that stretched farther than the last pair of size eight jeans I'd tried to pull on over my size ten hips, I finally said the only thing that came to mind. "I get migraines, and strange objects seem to follow me around." I cringed inwardly. As random statements went, it was somewhere in the realm of "I see dead people."

To my shock, Alice cocked her head, narrowed her small eyes behind the massive glasses, and smiled. "Well now, that's just perfect. Okay then. Let's get started."

2

BLAH, BLAH, BLAH, WATCH OUT!

I stood just inside the door, aware on some level of Alice puttering around the massive space, chatting aimlessly and pointing out objects here and there which she deemed important for me to notice.

My eyes felt like they might bulge out of my face. My mouth hung open and I was rooted to the spot, my bright red sneakers glued to the concrete floor from the feeling of being totally overwhelmed.

"...sit in that chair over there," Alice was saying when my mind refocused. "It belonged to Casanova and...blah, blah, blah..."

Good idea, I thought. Sit down, I told myself. *Before you fall.* I reached back and my fingers found the glossy, curved arms of the ancient chair. I all but fell into it. For a moment the well-worn upholstery wrapped around my body, embracing me with an almost human warmth. I settled into the embrace with a sigh, a sense of pure joy filling me as I realized I'd found a place where I felt perfectly at home.

Not the chair. But, the enormous room arrayed before me, filled with magical objects.

I was in heaven.

Then the seat beneath me shifted. I shifted too, frowning as it rolled beneath my flesh. "What in the world...?"

Something pinched my right butt cheek. Hard.

I leaped out of the chair with a squeal of surprise, rubbing my assaulted cheek and glaring at the chair. To my amazement, the stupid piece of ancient furniture leaped off the floor and danced from leg to leg, looking for all the world as if it were celebrating.

A series of snorts sounded behind me. "I told you not to sit in that chair," Alice said, shaking her head. "First rule of being a Keeper of the Artifacts, don't touch anything you don't understand." She wandered away again, mouth moving and arms flailing to point from object to object without apparent order or plan.

I followed along behind her, my thoughts spinning as I tried to grasp the rapid-fire information she was flinging at me.

Something clattered to the floor behind me and I jumped, whirling around with a yelp of surprise. A colorful ball of ratty-looking feathers cartwheeled through the air and smacked into me, hitting me between my breasts with an outraged squawk.

"Arrrrrghhhh!" It yelled into my face. "Avast ye blackguard, for Blackbeard's sword will take yer head in one, two..."

Alice's hand snapped out and snatched a deadly looking blade out of the air, inches from my nose.

"...Three!" finished the parrot gleefully. "Shiver me timbers, it's a pirate's life and a bottle o' rum. The lads'll have some bleepin' fun!"

I shoved the horrible creature away. He flew off with a cackle, feathers raining down on our heads as he fluttered above us in a messy circle.

Alice expelled a frustrated breath. "You do attract trouble, don't you, sweetums?" She threw the blade into the air and fired a silvery ribbon of magic at it. Quick as a snake, the energy wrapped itself around the blade and dragged it toward the nearest enormous shelving unit, settling it down onto the top shelf.

A heavy black projectile leaped from the big wooden desk near the stairs, claws unsheathed as it swiped at the fluttering parrot. The cat barely missed the bird's tangle of ratty feathers. A fresh spate of moth-eaten red and green feathers drifted into the air as the parrot rolled sideways in midair to evade the big cat's claws.

Fenwald landed far more lightly than I would have expected, given his size, and trotted across the artifact library, flopping to his side in a beam of sunlight that painted the floor in happy stripes.

With another outraged squawk and several more bleeps, the parrot followed the sword to the top of the shelves and settled down next to it. In a blink, it had lowered its head and seemed to be sleeping.

"Did that bird just swear at us?"

Alice sighed. "I'm afraid so. He lived with pirates all his life and talks like a sailor. I brought a witch in to hex him with a magical bleeping spell. Nasty critter."

"Does he have a name?" I asked, eyeing his suspiciously still form.

"No idea. I call him Parrot."

"Fenwald, come on handsome kitty." Alice bared her teeth at me, making me flinch. After a beat, I realized it was her version of a smile. "I'm off to fix beans for lunch. You coming?"

"That sounds...um...yes. Give me a minute?" I just wanted a few minutes by myself to try to make sense of something Alice had shared with me during the morning. I lifted my notebook, which was filled with half-written words, squiggly lines and sentences that trailed off into nothing as I'd tried to keep up with my teacher's rapid-fire teaching style. "I'm just going to make some notes."

"Brilliant! I'll give you a shout when lunch is ready."

As she disappeared through the door that

divided the public-facing bookstore from the "Librarian Only" magical area, I gave a sigh of relief.

I stood in front of an oversized desk and looked around at the immediate area, taking in the enormity of the task ahead of me. The room was bisected by two rows of enormous shelves with a narrow aisle between them. Each shelving unit reached thirty feet above my head, still nowhere near the ceiling, which looked to be at least fifty feet high and sported several enormous fans that slowly stirred the air in the massive room. Each fan had a light fixture attached, but none of them were on, yet the room was filled with light. Given the enormity of the magical inventory in the place, most of it probably as ancient as time, I'd have expected a stale smell, maybe even moldy and sour, like old furniture or aged books. But the air was as fresh as a sunny day.

And, unlike the bookstore, the huge space was the perfect temperature.

Directly across from the entrance to the store in front, was a garage-sized door that I assumed was used for oversized artifacts. Twenty yards in front of that door was a long, wooden table, which was covered with more artifacts, some of them in a jumble.

Alice had said something about the artifacts on that table not being cataloged yet.

I stood in the center of the space and lifted my gaze, turning slowly to take it all in. There had to be thousands, maybe millions of things on the shelves. They kept on going and going into the seemingly endless depths of the place.

And I needed to learn about every single artifact. Every. Single. One.

I was doomed.

With that daunting thought, I turned to the table of uncatalogued items. If I had to memorize every item in the place, I'd better get started.

And that table seemed like a great place to start.

A truly horrendous smell filled the air around me. I waved a hand under my nose and grimaced toward the dividing door. What was Alice cooking?.

I stared at the pair of woman's shoes I'd been cataloging and blinked, trying to dispel the shadows wreathing their otherwise harmless-looking forms. I touched one of the shoes with a fingertip and felt a subtle vibration saturating the cloth, the sensation filling me with an inexplicable unease.

I wished I knew how to read the artifacts. But I had a feeling it would take time and a lot more learning before I got to that point.

Despite the horrible stench of whatever Alice was cooking, I was getting hungry. My stomach rumbled loudly.

I set the shoes aside, deciding to ask Alice about them after lunch.

My gaze fell on the next item on the table. It was a suitcase that looked like it had been stuffed with cabbages. There was a large grease spot on the top, and the semi-rigid sides bulged unnaturally. There were gaps around the edges where it appeared that the suitcase hadn't entirely closed.

It looked old.

Like about a hundred years old.

"Oy! Naida, I've got beans and bangers," Alice called out.

Bangers? I assumed bangers were some kind of British food, but they didn't sound very appetizing. Smoothing my expression to neutral, I lifted a hand. "I'll be right there." No wonder the place stunk so badly, I thought. Anything called bangers had to be terrible.

Fenwald bumped against my calves with an engine purr that could have powered a Ferrari. I looked down at him. "Hey, Fenny. Any advice on whether I should eat the bangers?"

"Meow," he told me, noncommittally.

"You're no help at all," I grumped. I gave him a scratch. "If it looks terrible, I'll just take your example and fling it into the corner when she's not looking."

"Meow," he agreed.

He jumped up onto the table and started sniffing around the suitcase, pawing at the bulging bag.

"Don't mess with the artifacts," I told him, setting my pad aside. "I've almost got them all organized."

"Meow!"

With a sigh, I headed for the store. A long feather flew off the shelves and lodged itself into my hair. With a sigh, I reached up and tugged it out, giving it a chastising glance. "None of that now, you have an assigned spot. You're supposed to stay there unless I call you."

The feather rippled gently, quivering in my hand. I narrowed my gaze on it. "What's your magic, anyway?"

The tip wasn't covered in ink, so I assumed it hadn't been used as a quill. A flowery scent filled my nostrils, and I grinned. "Woman's hat, huh? I think you need to get back to it then."

I opened my hand and gave my fingers a little twitch in the direction of the artifact shelving. "Go on now."

The feather lifted from my palm, did a little shimmy, and then dusted my nose with its soft barbs before dancing through the air to the spot on the shelves where a woman's hat from centuries past waited. The hat was covered in plastic, no doubt sealed, but somehow the little feather had wriggled its way free to visit me.

I smiled, giving it a little wave before heading toward my bangers and beans.

If I survived lunch, I'd try to get the story on the hat feather.

Alice settled a wide, shallow bowl in front of me. I looked down at a pale glop of beans with a fat sausage sitting on top. "She grinned happily. "Tuck in, now. We've oodles of work ahead today."

I glanced longingly toward the dividing door, wishing I could get back to my cataloging. I felt curiously competent when I was dealing with the artifacts. As if I'd been meant to work with them all along.

Maybe I had.

I took a bite of the pale-colored beans and forced myself to smile at Alice. She was watching me for my reaction. "Good, yeah?"

I swallowed quickly and nodded. "Delicious."

Something dinged and she jumped up. "Brilliant! The bread's done."

I shoved the pasty, tasteless beans around my plate, wishing Alice had a dog I could surreptitiously feed under the table. "I've been cataloging the artifacts on the table in the back," I told her.

She glanced up, humming her response. I

watched as she settled a beautiful, golden loaf of bread onto another cat-decorated towel and dug in the drawer for a knife.

"I'm almost done with them," I said. I was hoping she'd be happy about my taking the initiative. But she seemed too engrossed in trying to get the knife to cut through the loaf of bread to pay attention. She hummed again, leaning all her weight on the knife.

It barely dented the bread's surface.

She stood back, wiping her hands on her apron, which I noticed was also covered in black cats, none of which bore even the slightest resemblance to the mountain-lion sized Fenwald. "I'll just let the bread rest a few minutes," she finally said. "The fibers need to loosen."

I fought a smile. She sat down across from me, cutting into the sausage and taking a tidy bite. "This brings me back to Sunday meals with my mums and gram," she said, smiling.

"That sounds nice," I told her.

She gave me a sideways glance as she scooped up beans. "Did your family have any special meals?"

The way she asked the question made me think she was fishing for information. I'd asked A.P. not to tell Alice any more about my family situation than he had to. I was embarrassed by my lack of magical upbringing, and mortified by the fact that I hadn't grown up with parents.

"My grandma liked roast beef with carrots and potatoes," I told her, keeping my tone neutral.

Alice held my gaze for a moment, no doubt noting my lack of enthusiasm. Finally, she nodded. "Brilliant. I'll be sure not to fix that."

I snorted out a surprised laugh.

She was intuitive. I'd have to remember that.

To thank her for her kindness, I admitted, "I like tacos and egg rolls."

"Good enough."

We ate in slightly awkward silence for a few minutes.

"I was wondering if you knew the story on that woman's hat with the rogue feather?"

Alice put her fork down. "Has that silly thing been a bother?"

I shook my head and set my fork into my nearly empty bowl. To my amazement, the banger hadn't been all that bad. "It came to see me. But I'm used to that. It's no bother."

She nodded. "You've got a unique attraction for magical objects. They probably sense your unformed magic. I suspect it's been a bit of a challenge at times?"

I grimaced. "Living with a non-magic grandma, it was more than a challenge."

"I've known the type. She pretended magic didn't exist?"

It was hard to explain. "Not so much that as..." I

pushed beans around in my bowl. "It took me a while to put a finger on it. The magic made her sad. I have no idea why, but it got to the point where I'd do anything to keep that look off her face." I looked at Alice. "I don't want you to think Grandma Neely was mean to me. She never was. She was kind and thoughtful in her own way. But something or someone hurt her badly once. She would never tell me. And she just couldn't find it in herself to help me embrace my magic. So the two of us played parts for the twenty years we lived together. We both pretended there was no such thing as magic. And I pretended I was happy about it." I shrugged. "It's not a big deal. I don't have much magic anyway."

Alice gave me a long look, her expression unreadable. Then she sighed, sitting back in her chair. "That's a cockup for sure. Well, we do need to get you up to speed. Until we do, you're going to keep having magical leakages."

I felt my eyebrows lifting. "Leakages?"

"Yes. These objects aren't coming to you of their own volition. You're calling them to you."

"But, I don't have any keeper magic." I felt my face go white. I hadn't meant to admit that to her.

"Of course you do, sweetums. It's raw and elemental, but it's there. We just need to teach you how to use it properly."

She was wrong. I wasn't inherently magical. I'd had twenty-two years to come to grips with that. But

I didn't argue. The last thing I wanted was to convince her of my unworthiness. The longer she believed I had promise, the longer she'd let me stay at Croakies.

And I really wanted to stay at Croakies. More than I'd wanted anything in my life.

Alice's gaze slid back to the brick that was shaped like a golden loaf of bread. "Well, I should get that sliced up and put away, or it'll get hard."

I pressed my lips together, gathering up my bowl so she couldn't see me smile. "I'll do the dishes."

"Brilliant." Alice headed toward the dividing door. "I'll be right back. I believe I've got just the blade in the back for slicing this bread."

I almost asked her if she meant Blackbeard's sword but bit back the tease, not sure how she'd take it.

It turned out her idea was worse anyway.

"I'm certain Jack's scalpel will be just the thing," she murmured as she opened the door.

My eyes bugging, I watched her disappear.

Surely she didn't mean Jack the Ripper's scalpel? Did she?

3

CROAKIES OR BUST!

I left Alice to dismember...erm...slice the bread and returned to my artifact logging.

Alice had told me I could look up the origin and purpose of each artifact by using Shakespeare's desk, but I'd been too intimidated to try it. However, with a full belly and no desire to be anywhere near Jack the Ripper's bread slicer, I decided it was as good a time as any to brave it.

I decided to start with the pair of women's shoes I'd cataloged last. The shoes looked brand new. The soles were spotless, the two-inch heels solid, and the pink cloth uppers pristine. They didn't look as if they'd ever been worn. Which was surprising to me. The magical artifacts I'd handled to that point had all obviously been around a while. Many of them were ancient. Their age like a fine patina that had a definite feel against my skin. With that patina came a vibration I'd always noticed when touching magical objects. Latent energy.

The shoes had no latent magical energy that I could sense. I couldn't help wondering if Alice had brought them to the library by mistake.

Getting slightly desperate, I searched the table again. I didn't see the shoes.

Fenwald was lying on top of the bumpy suitcase, bathing himself. The stench I'd noticed before, that I'd attributed to Alice's cooking, still hung in the area. I waved a hand under my nose. "Is that you, Fenny?"

The big cat stopped bathing to look at me, his entire body vibrating with disgust.

"Sorry," I said, eyeing him for signs that he was considering retribution. "I didn't mean to disparage your hygiene."

After glaring at me for another minute, he went back to bathing.

I sighed. "I know I put those shoes right here." I moved a few things around, but the shoes weren't there. "Humbug on a high heel!" I murmured. "I'm losing my mind."

"Meow!" Fenny agreed enthusiastically.

"Button it, fuzzy butt."

A soft chime pulled my attention around. I frowned as a sheet of paper drifted to the floor behind me. "What in the...?"

The dividing door slammed open, and Alice

hurried through. Her expression was intense, and she still had the scalpel clutched in her hand.

Uh oh, I thought. *She's been possessed by the spirit of Jack the Ripper. I knew that scalpel was gonna be trouble!*

"Why am I getting *that* order again?" she asked, looking confused.

I was pretty sure she wasn't talking to me. But I was the only one in the room, so I shrugged.

"Meow!" Fenny said, just in case she'd been directing the question his way.

"Here, sweetums, hold this for me, yeah? Cheers." Handing me the deadly blade, Alice grabbed the sheet of paper off the floor, scanning it quickly. "Harridan hijinks!" she muttered.

"What is that?" I asked.

"An artifact wrangling order. I'm to repossess a pair of magical heels. But I already retrieved those." She slapped the sheet of paper down on the table and glanced around, shoving things to the side in growing agitation. "They were just here."

"The shoes?" I asked, stalling for time.

"Yes. Did you put them somewhere?"

"No. I was just looking for them myself. They were right there," I pointed to a small empty spot on the table. "...when I went to lunch."

Alice sighed. "Well, that's it then. It's into the toxic vault for them once we've retrieved them again." She looked at me. "This will be a good first retrieval for you."

All the blood ran out of my body and settled onto the floor. "Um, Yikes! I've only been here half a day..."

"Pshaw!" she said by way of argument. "You'll do fine. Just call the police..." Alice dug into all her pockets, including the ones in her banger-stained apron, and finally came up with a dingy, battered card. "This is our man on the inside. Tell him what we're looking for and that you're my apprentice. He'll keep you on the straight and narrow."

She grabbed the blade back out of my nerveless fingers. "Off you go then."

"I..." My lips flapped. "I..." I reached for her as she hurried away. "Um...I..."

"See that you're back in time for dinner. I'm thinking of making Haggis tonight. You're going to love it!"

———

Detective Wise Grym was built like a brick wall. Granted, the wall was man-shaped and very attractive, but it was still a wall. Around six feet tall, the irritated-looking detective had broad shoulders, dark-caramel eyes, and mahogany brown hair that was bleached with golden streaks where the sun had kissed it. His square jaw and sharply cut cheekbones could have been carved from stone. In fact, at that moment, they looked sharp enough to cut yours truly into tiny little pieces.

Like an angry, man-shaped version of Jack's blade.

"What do you mean, they disappeared?" he asked me again. Since he'd walked into Croakies, his handsome face filled with an expression of what could only be called impatient weariness, he'd asked me the same question couched a variety of ways no fewer than five times.

We were going nowhere. Repeatedly.

"Like I've said five times now, they were sitting on the table when I went to eat lunch, and when I came back, they were gone."

Hands on hips, gaze hostile, and lips pressed tight in disgust, the detective seemed to think I had something to do with the missing shoes. Maybe he thought I'd taken them myself.

"I can promise you I didn't steal them," I told him, just in case his beady little brain was dancing that particular chicken dance.

Grym lifted his gaze from the ugly carpet. He eyed me for a long moment and then sighed. The expulsion of air seemed to take some of the starch out of his sails. "I'd hoped those stupid shoes were in my rearview mirror."

"You've dealt with them before?" I asked, frowning.

"Unfortunately. They've killed three women so far. And they were nearly impossible to get hold of the first time." He shook his head. "Don't you people have some kind of magical holding cell or something? Those shoes are toxic."

I didn't know if we had one of those or not. But there was no way I was telling him that. "Of course we do. But we didn't even get past the cataloging stage before they disappeared."

He glared down at me. "Maybe next time you can secure them first and *then* fill out your paperwork."

I glared right back, too stupid to know when I was beaten.

Behind me, the dividing door opened and closed. "Oy, Grymsie!"

The detective glanced at Alice, his gaze narrowing on her as I turned. "What's that in your hair?" he asked.

She shook her head, the wild nest of graying brown curls dancing happily with the action. "What? Did I pick up that devil's spawn of a feather again?" She patted the curly mass, her fingers repeatedly missing the Christmas-colored critter dancing through the strands.

I squinted at it. "What is that thing?"

Alice's confusion cleared. "You mean Oliver?"

She laughed gaily. "He's a magical tree frog. Isn't he gorgeous?"

I grimaced as she plucked him from her hair. The little critter blinked at us through round, black eyes, his tiny fingers?...claws?...talons?...clutching Alice's hand.

"What does it do?" I asked, trying not to grimace. I was so not a frog person. Although he was kind of cute. In an ugly sort of way.

Alice peered rather intently at the frog. It blinked back at her. "I'm not sure," she finally said. "The Quillerans sold him to me. They said he was very special, and that he would one day reveal his magic to me."

I nodded as if that made perfect sense. Though, I was pretty sure she'd been taken for a magical mystery tour on that one.

Grym shook his head. "It's never dull here, is it?"

Alice gave her peculiar snorting laugh. "Not for a minute. You two suss out the shoe problem?"

"There's no sussing to do, I'm afraid," Grym told the Keeper. "I'll have to start hitting all the women's shoe stores again. If it's like the last time, it'll take me days to find them. Hopefully, we'll get them before they kill someone else." He sighed. "I don't have time for this. We've had a rash of unexplained robberies in Enchanted, and I'm supposed to be solving that right now."

"How can a pair of shoes kill someone?" I asked,

immediately regretting my question as Grym turned a hostile gaze in my direction.

"They carry the wearer into the street and get them run over by a passing vehicle."

"Ugh..." My instincts were spot-on. It *had* been an unfortunate question. And his answer made me wonder why Alice hadn't been more careful with the things. Feeling responsible for their loss, even though there'd been no way for me to know how dangerous they were, I opened my mouth and offered something I really shouldn't have. "I'll help you find them."

Gulp!

What have I done? "I mean, I feel bad about losing them. I'd like to help you look." That sounded suitably harmless, right?

Grym stared at me for a long moment and then, to my everlasting surprise, nodded. "Can you get these things to come to you when we find them?"

I opened my mouth to tell him that I had no idea. But Alice cut me off. "She's my apprentice. Of course, she can."

I slid Alice a wide-eyed look and she smiled. "Go on with you then. No time like the present for getting a little street experience."

I followed Detective Grym out of Croakies feeling as if I was in an alternate universe. I was one day into my apprenticeship and already buried up to my nostrils in trouble.

The crabby cop pointed to a plain black SUV sitting at the curb down from Croakies. "This is me."

The door of the shop next door opened, and a curvy woman with light brown hair streaked in blonde highlights came outside carrying a broom. The woman had beautiful turquoise eyes and wore a plain white tee shirt with a long, pale green skirt that danced around her shapely legs as she walked. She smiled at me and called out to Grym. "Detective. Is everything all right?"

He lifted a hand. "Nothing I can't handle Ms. Coleman."

I ran my gaze over the name of her shop, which was emblazoned in gold letters across the plate glass window of the front. *Herbal Remedies with Mystical Properties.*

I made myself a promise to drop in for a visit soon to introduce myself. From the looks of the woman's aura, she had magical power of some kind. And I wanted to know what kind.

I blinked at the thought, realizing I could see her aura. It was shimmering, pale green color like her frothy skirt.

I'd never been able to see auras before. Hadn't even known what an aura looked like. The newly discovered skill was surprising. And icy. Once I got over the thrill of it, I wondered what the color meant.

"Ms. Griffith? Are you coming?" Detective Grym

had rolled down the passenger side window and was calling me like a naughty pooch. His manner suddenly irritated me. So I deliberately offered the woman my hand. "Hello, I'm Naida Griffith."

"Leandra Coleman. But my friends call me Lea. It's a pleasure to meet you. Do you work with Detective Grym?" As she asked the question, her gaze slid over my jeans and tee-shirt, the latter of which I realized with horror had an oily stain on the front from banger juice. "No. I'm in training next door. I'd like to chat sometime soon. If it's all right with you?"

Lea's ocean-tinted gaze sparkled with pleasure. "I'd love that. Stop by anytime."

"Ms. Griffith, I'm leaving without you if you don't step it up."

I rolled my eyes and the other woman laughed, the sound light and carefree. "I'll see you again," she told me, waving at Detective Grumpy Pants before starting to sweep the sidewalk in front of her store.

I climbed into the car, feeling happy with myself for having made the connection. "She's nice."

Grym grunted noncommittally.

I scanned him a look, narrowing my gaze in an effort to read his aura. There was a slight, grayish shimmer encompassing his big form, but nothing like the shimmering lightness surrounding Lea.

He caught me staring. "What?"

"Nothing." I wasn't exactly up-to-speed on supernormal etiquette, but I was pretty sure it would be considered rude to come right out and ask him what species of magic user he was. He was probably some kind of shifter. Judging by how prickly he was, probably a porcupine. I grinned at the thought. "Where are we going?" I asked.

"There are three shoe shops and two department type stores in Enchanted. We'll start with those. Hopefully, we'll get lucky."

I nodded. "That shouldn't take too long."

He glanced over at me, giving me a pitying look. "You wouldn't think so, would you?"

I frowned. "I'm sensing that you disagree?"

He sighed. "They can smell a predator a mile away. They were spelled by a black witch and given a sort of innate intelligence. The last time I searched for them, they kept ducking out of every store I entered and returning to the first store I'd looked to throw me off. If the shoes are hiding in a stock room somewhere, we'll have to go through every single box looking for them. If they've already been purchased, we'll have to chase the buyer down, hopefully before she succumbs to the siren's song of the shoes. And then there's the worst-case scenario..."

I couldn't imagine what would be worse than going through every single shoebox in the back room of five different stores. "What's that?"

"If the shoes managed to find a wearer without even going to a store."

I realized he was right. For all we knew, they could have thrown themselves down in front of someone walking down the sidewalk. If I found a pretty pair of shoes that looked new, abandoned on the sidewalk, I would definitely pick them up. I was sure I wasn't alone on that.

"At least they're limited to only women who wear that size," I offered helpfully.

The pity in his gaze deepened. "Wrong again. The shoes will size themselves to the wearer's feet."

Of course they would. I thought bitterly.

Grym narrowed his eyes on me. "How long have you been working with artifacts?" His inference was clear. He was asking me why I knew so little about how things worked in the supernormal world.

I shrugged. "I wasn't raised by supernormals."

Just when I thought he couldn't find me any more pathetic, he looked at me as if I were a one-armed blind woman trying to tie her shoes.

We sat in uncomfortable silence for most of the short trip. I tried to break the tension once by asking about his robbery case. But he didn't seem to want to talk about it. All he would reveal was that the police couldn't figure out how the thieves were getting into the banks and jewelry stores they were robbing.

By the time the detective finally pulled into a small, paved lot on a quaint, cobblestoned street in the market section of Enchanted, I was considering just opening my door and flinging myself out onto the cobblestones.

The detective wasn't driving all that fast. Maybe I'd even survive.

"Okay," he said. "Fortunately, two of the target stores are on this street."

I followed his lead and climbed out of the car.

Grym pointed to a shop called *The Cobbler's Heels* and glared down at me. "I'll take the lead. I just need you to quietly throw out your Keeper magic to see if the shoes are there."

I swallowed hard, nodding.

Alice had briefly explained how that worked, but we hadn't practiced it yet. She'd told me the skill was a second week of training kind of thing. It had seemed like the most important skill of all to me. I'd attempted to argue with her, but she'd plowed on to the next item on her personal slave list before I could utter a single word.

With the sun shining high overhead and a flower-scented breeze wafting over us from the enormous pots of flowers along the street, I realized the boondoggle with the detective was actually a vast improvement on dusting shelves and checking tags with Alice.

My dusting skills had never been all that great anyway.

4

FLIP FLOPPED WITH EXTREME PREJUDICE

"Can I help you?" a soft female voice asked when we entered the shop.

We'd been to all the possible stores and had spent hours searching for the shoes, finding nothing. We'd begun to suspect that the shoes had returned to the first shop we'd searched, as they had the last time Grym had looked for them, and we'd returned to that shop hoping to catch them unaware.

Grym headed for the sales girl, who gave him a bright smile. "You're back. Are you thinking of buying those boots after all?"

I left him to it and headed into the woman's side of the store. Despite a frustrating day of searching, I still moved toward the shelves of shoes like a zombie heading for fresh brains.

Shoes were my drug of choice. Aside from egg rolls, tacos, and anything sweet and fattening, shoes were my biggest weakness. I walked along the shelves of strappy sandals, my fingers reaching out to reverently touch each one. I sighed with happiness and then moved toward the heels. A moment later, I stiffened when a large form heated the air behind me and cleared its throat.

I turned and gave Grym a stiff smile. "Haven't found them yet."

He arched a pair of dark brows. I was beginning to suspect he was on to me and my shoe fetish. "You'll need to use your Keeper magic. As we discussed before, they can change their appearance and even their size, so a visual search won't work."

I pressed my lips together to keep from sticking my tongue out at him. Pulling my shoulders back, I opted instead for more adult behavior. "I was just getting ready to do that."

He nodded. "Do the back room too." He walked around the shelves blocking me from the sales lady's view and returned to the young woman with a smile that made her flush with pleasure.

I looked at her with a shocked expression. Who would smile like that at Detective Crabby Pants? The poor woman must be desperate for a boyfriend. On the plus side, when he left her sobbing into her sushi, she had a vast array of options for shoe therapy right in front of her.

I forced my attention back to the task at hand. At

least his interest was pointed elsewhere, and that was good for me.

I closed my eyes and tried to feel the energy waiting deep inside my core. I concentrated hard, trying to shove the sound of the flirting across the store out of my consciousness. It wasn't easy.

I mean, ignoring the flirting.

Well, finding my Keeper magic wasn't easy either.

But the flirting made me kind of sick.

I belched softly.

Nope, that was the banger coming back for a visit. I grimaced. It didn't taste nearly as good the second time.

"Were you looking for anything specific?" the girl asked Detective Grouchy Britches.

I twitched, realizing I'd gotten distracted from my task.

My energy wilted like a plucked dandelion in the hot sun.

I shoved air out of my lungs, shook my hands as if trying to loosen them, and then closed my eyes again, searching for the core of my power.

Nothing.

Except for a hard knot in my belly, which I suspected was lunch.

Using my Keeper magic wasn't coming easily to me. It had gotten a tiny bit easier each time I tried, but I was still far from good at it.

Something touched my shoulder. I jumped with a yelp and swung around.

A delicate pair of sandals hung in the air in front of me. The sun beyond the glass found the pink crystals arranged at the top of the shoes and sparked with vibrant energy.

The rogue shoes had found me. I must have leaked again. For once, my leakage had come in handy. "Well, hello there," I murmured softly.

A tiny part of my brain reminded me that the shoes were dangerous.

But they were so pretty.

My hands came up, my gaze locked on the dainty sandals. As I looked at them, they gave a happy little dance and shot toward the floor, positioning themselves in front of my feet. All I had to do was slip off my sneakers and...

"Yes, the more tread, the better," a loud male voice said.

My gaze jerked toward Grym and I found him staring at me over the woman's bent form as she dug into her supply of men's boots.

I shook my head to clear it of the shoes' magical influence, but he seemed to take that as a denial that I'd found them. He pointed impatiently toward the open door behind the sales counter. Through the wide crack between a pair of white curtains, I could see rows and rows of shoe boxes, stacked from the floor all the way to the ceiling.

I grimaced.

My gaze was caught by movement down by my feet. The sandals were shifting color, their pretty jeweled uppers sifting through the rainbow from pink to white, to turquoise blue, to violet, to...

I forced myself into action, shoving away the magical muzziness I didn't doubt the shoes were causing in my brain.

Either that, or I was suffering from banger poisoning.

Hm...

I bent double, reaching for the shoes. "Come to me, my pretties," I mumbled.

Something in my voice or expression must have warned them that I meant trouble.

They jerked out of my grasp and hung in the air for a moment, shifting with the light to cast pretty shapes over the nearby shelves with their crystals. Watching the shapes, I felt my mind going muzzy again.

I gave myself a hard shake, one hand snaking out to grab a shoe out of the air.

As soon as my fingers closed around it, the thing went spastic.

It shot skyward, taking my hand with it. I barely held on as the shoe tried to yank away from my grip, the other sandal pummeling me about the head and shoulders.

I tried to grab the second shoe, but it dodged

neatly away. Before my eyes, the things turned into high heels again. They were a deep, blood-red color with four-inch-tall metallic heels that looked painfully sharp.

I quickly learned just how sharp they were when the rogue shoe started attacking me, heel first.

"Ahhh!" I screamed as the heel bit into my throat and then danced away before I could wrap a hand around it.

The shoe in my other hand stopped trying to pull out of my grip and suddenly shot toward me, catching me off guard. The heel hit me between the eyes and agony ripped through me.

Fear turned to rage. I swung my hand at the errant shoe and blasted it with a slender gray ribbon of energy.

The wimpy shot of power wrapped around the flailing stiletto and gripped it tight, the artifact shifting colors again as it fought to get free.

The delicate high heel turned to a heavy boot. The loose shoe...boot...launched itself at my head, kicking me right in the temple. I went down, shrieking Grym's name as the one shoe I'd managed to grab wrenched itself from my grip.

Despite the dizziness left behind by the violence of the attack, I started to shove myself back to my feet. There was a jangling sound, and I realized someone had come through the front door. My first thought was that the shoes were going to escape through the door.

I stumbled upward. But it appeared the shoes were vengeful. They contented themselves instead with wailing on me, serving up an energetic boot to the belly, one to the thigh, and a couple to my forearms as I tried to defend myself against the attack.

Just as I believed I wasn't going to survive the attack, a big hand whipped out of nowhere and wrapped around one of the boots.

Grym fought the boot, almost losing it when it shifted from a bulky walking boot to a slender flip flop, finally managing to shove it into a bag unlike any I'd ever seen before and seal it in. The shoe immediately stopped fighting, the bag quieting, and Grym dropped it to the floor as he reached for the second flip flop.

Not a moment too soon.

The stupid thing hung in the air like a sparkly featherweight boxer, slapping me on one cheek and then the other so quickly I couldn't get a hand on it as my head was thrown from side to side. Pain was a constant torment over my face, head and neck and stars danced before my gaze.

Grym grasped the angry flip flop and shoved it into a second bag before it could shift to a thigh-high biker boot and beat us both into carpet stains.

I sagged back against the shelves, my entire body throbbing with pain, blood running from my stiletto wounds, and my chest heaving. I was so not in shape for fieldwork.

Grym winced when he eyed me. "You okay?"

I couldn't help myself, I gave him the evil eye. "Do I look okay?"

He shrugged. "Not really. But I'm sure that was pretty par for the course in your job, eh?"

Holy Humperdink! I thought. I certainly hoped not.

Detective Grym dropped me off at Croakies, nodding at me as I clasped the door and shoved it open. "Ms. Griffith, I appreciate your help."

I grimaced as I turned in my seat, every muscle in my body sore. It had been a mistake to sit still for so long. "It was my..." I grimaced, putting a hand to my lower back like an old woman. "...pleasure."

He made a sound that was suspiciously like a laugh, I turned to glare at him. "Don't forget these." He shoved the two bags at me. "Tell Alice to put them under nullifying magic and behind a locked door. And keep them separated."

I took the bags, feeling the magic vibrating through the thick plastic. I didn't know enough to discern if the energy was from the shoes or from the specially magicked bags that held them. "I will."

I started to close the door.

"Ms. Griffith?"

I stopped, leaning down to look into the car before I remembered my entire body was broken. Pain sliced through me, and I winced before I could stop myself. "Yes?"

"Can I see your phone?"

I frowned, my hand hovering protectively over the cell phone in my pocket. "Why?"

He held out a hand, impatiently wiggling the fingers.

I stared at him for a few beats and then sighed, handing it to him. He was, after all, the long arm of the law.

Grym tapped a few buttons and handed it back to me. "In case you need to get in touch. It's my direct line."

I looked down to find that he'd stored his number as a Favorite. Cheeky. Embarrassingly, he was my *only* Favorite. "Thanks."

"For what it's worth, I think it was a dirty trick sending you out into the field before you're trained. You could have been badly injured."

Since I'd been stabbed by stilettos, beaten by a boot, and flogged by flip flops, I couldn't imagine what he considered *badly* injured. Maybe it required a limb being sawed off. "I can handle myself."

The detective was looking at me with pity again.

I hated it when someone looked at me that way. It made me feel inadequate.

"I'm not completely untrained," I objected. I'd thought I'd functioned reasonably well for my first day on the job.

He stared at me. "Look, what you're doing... training to become a Keeper...it's a dangerous job. You're playing with fire attempting it without any knowledge. I wanted you to know that I won't bring you out with me again until you're trained. If Alice won't come, then the KoA won't be involved in the next takedown. It's not my job to train you, and I don't want to see you get hurt."

Again...stabbed, bludgeoned, flogged.

I glared at him, so offended by his statement that I couldn't respond. He gave me a little wave and then pulled away from the curb, driving off down the street before it occurred to me that I'd just been insulted and dismissed in one, long breath.

"Gnish!" I called after him, mentally kicking myself for being stupid.

I should have laid him out.

Turning around, I hobbled toward Croakies. The door to the herbal shop opened and Lea poked her head out. "Are you okay?"

I realized I was walking as if I were a hundred years old and tried to straighten, so I didn't look so pathetic. "Sure. I'm good."

Lea narrowed her startling blue eyes on me. "I

don't think so. Come on inside. I'll brew you a special tea that will make you feel better."

I shook my head. "I really should get these inside..."

She came out onto the sidewalk, wrapping an arm around my shoulders. "Don't be silly. They're fine for a few minutes. Come on. You're making me hurt to look at you."

I threw a glance at Croakies and balanced the need to unburden myself of the killer shoes against the desire for the help and kindness the other woman promised. "Maybe just for a few minutes," I said.

"Good." She offered me her hand. "I think I might have some muffins too. We'll make it a little tea party."

5

UM...IS THERE COFFEE?

It turned out that Lea was easy to talk to. By the time we'd consumed two cups of tea and as many muffins apiece, she was wiping tears of laughter from her face from my retelling of being shoe mugged.

Lea got up for a tissue, drying her face and blowing her nose. "Oh my goddess, that's hilarious."

I grinned at her, feeling much better as her special tea worked its way into my system and made everything feel better. Including my mood. "It was touch and go there for a while," I admitted.

Then I remembered what Grym had said to me, and my smile slid away. "Detective Grym wasn't impressed by my methods. He told me he wouldn't ride with me again."

Lea's expression turned to annoyance. "That

wasn't very kind..." she said, running a fingertip along the rim of her teacup.

I sensed a "but" in there, so I cut it off at the pass. "But you think he was right?"

"Not to take it up with you, no. I'd say you did the best you could under the circumstances. It's not a criticism of you. But Alice should have known better."

I knew she was right. But I couldn't help feeling as if I was a failure. Shaking my head, I said, "I should have known more about how my magic worked when I took the job."

Lea fixed me with a kind look. I hadn't told her about my upbringing. Not the whole story. I'd just glossed quickly over it, too embarrassed to admit how little my parents apparently cared about me to leave me with someone who wouldn't help me with such an important part of my life.

I didn't even really know what had happened to them. All my grandma would tell me was that they'd both died when I was two years old.

Lea was looking at me as if she knew everything about my life. I'd known her less than an hour, but I was starting to understand that she was a very intuitive person. "We're all the product of our upbringing Naida. We can't control our situation. We're only responsible for what we make of it. I have a feeling you're going to make as much of this

Keeper gig as you can. That's all anybody can ask of you."

I nodded. Her words didn't give me a pass. In fact, they were kind of a challenge. In a nice way, she was telling me to pull up my big girl panties and be the best Keeper apprentice I could be. She was right. And it was just the kick in the knickers I needed.

I smiled. "I'm going to prove Detective Surly Shorts wrong if it kills me," I told her.

She grinned, her beautiful gaze sparkling with humor. "That a girl. Now, tell me about the flip flop slaps again. I don't think I'll ever get tired of hearing that one."

I lay on my cot in the big room and looked around, my eyes wide open. I'd been so tired when I'd hit the cot that I'd fallen quickly and deeply asleep. But then I'd had terrible dreams about men in old-fashioned uniforms exchanging bullets for arrows with a bunch of horseback riding Native Americans, and I'd jerked awake, the stench of gunpowder and the screams of charging men sifting through my mind.

My heart still pounding against my ribs from the dream, I shoved upright and looked around, the feeling of danger and death sliding away as the artifact library wrapped its soothing presence around me. Despite its massive size, the big space felt like home in a way my grandma's house never had.

Surrounded by thousands of magical artifacts, I felt as if I was among friends. As strange as that was. A soft breeze bathed my cheeks, and I looked up to find the hat feather that had visited me earlier, hanging in the air before me.

I smiled when it cocked itself to one side as if in question. "I'm okay." I shoved at the hard cot. "This is just really uncomfortable." It could be because my body was a study in bruise art from the shoe beating incident.

Those stupid flip flops had packed quite a punch. Literally.

The feather dipped and swirled across the air in front of me. Music swelled from nowhere, filling the space with an old-fashioned waltz that the feather seemed to like. The dancing artifact was soon joined by a pirouetting hat pin. The two of them dipped and soared through the dimly-lit space.

Watching them, I could almost envision two people dancing the waltz in a glittery ballroom. I laughed, enjoying the show.

With a soft sifting of air, the straw hat flew from its spot on the stacks and dropped onto my head. I went very still, blinking in surprise for a beat, and then felt myself beginning to move to the elegant notes of the Walz.

The notes grew and swelled, and I found myself

swaying with unaccustomed grace through the moves.

I laughed with delight as I frolicked to the music. Pleasure infused me. The music sped, and I moved faster and faster to keep up. My feet never missed a step. Rather than getting tired, I was intoxicated by the movement and the music.

The ribbons of the hat slipped around my throat, tying into a loose bow. I rejected the brief jolt of alarm as the bow fluffed loosely beneath my chin, offering grace and beauty rather than harm.

The first Walz moved into another and another, and my heart filled with the beauty of the experience. Even as my legs tired and my feet started to falter, I felt only pleasure. But my eyes began to droop, and my feet stopped feeling the floor. When I could barely keep moving from weariness, the feather slipped its soft barbs across my eyes and I dropped, hitting a floor that felt like a feather pillow rather than the concrete it was. My thoughts drifted into darkness as the music sang me to sleep.

I slept deeply until morning, not waking until someone made a loud throat-clearing sound. My eyes fluttered open and I stretched, enjoying the comfy cloud of my bed. But as soon as my eyes opened I felt the cold hardness of concrete beneath me.

Alice stared down at me, worry set deeply into her expression. The tiny frog in her hair peered at me from just above her left ear, its black gaze equally concerned.

Fenwald was stretched out next to me, batting at the hat feather I'd been clutching in one hand.

I shoved upright, dizziness making me wobble. "What happened? How did I get here?"

Alice's thin lips pressed together. "I'd say that's rather obvious, yeah?" She nodded toward the feather. "You let the magic grab hold of you. What were you thinking, Naida? You could have been seriously hurt."

Silky ribbons tugged against my throat. I looked down to where the hat ties were caught beneath my backside. I lifted one butt-cheek and pulled the ribbon free, reaching up to tug the hat off my head. I was alarmed to find the hatpin sticking into the back of the straw, no doubt just barely missing my scalp. "Oh. I..."

I dropped the feather inside the hat and rubbed my face. "I had a nightmare and couldn't go back to sleep. The feather was entertaining me."

Alice's gaze slid to the cot. "Oy! That's on me, I'm afraid. I forgot. That's Custer's cot."

Still half asleep, I was having trouble processing her words. "Custer? Who's that?"

"You know, Custer's Last Stand? The cot's a bit stuck in the past. Everyone who sleeps on it relives the battle. I am sorry, Naida." She cocked her head, and the tree frog scurried through the frizzy mass of her hair to peer at me from the top of her head. "You can sleep on my couch from now forwards if you'd like."

I didn't like that option any better, but I needed coffee before I made any decisions. Yawning, I pushed to my feet. "I'll just put this away."

Fenwald jumped up and trotted with me to the shelves and then followed me to the dividing door, yowling impatiently for me to open it. I stopped, blinking rapidly to clear the last of the sleep from my eyes. I glanced back to where Alice still stood. "Um, is there coffee?"

B arely managing to wriggle my way out of eating something called spotted dick for breakfast, I gnawed on a rock-hard scone from the day before, carefully scraping slivers from the end, so I didn't break my teeth.

I'd kill for a donut or two. My stomach rumbled enthusiastically at the thought.

Or maybe three.

The bell jangled on the front door, and I looked up from the notes I'd been reading to see a tiny, elderly woman with sparkling gray eyes come inside. She was brushing at her coat and tsking energetically.

I jumped up, eager for a break from my studies. "Hello."

The woman smiled at me, adjusting her handbag over her wrist. "Hello, dear. You're new."

I nodded, "I'm Naida," I said, offering her my hand and immediately feeling silly for having done it. But she clasped my offering in a soft grip.

"It's nice to meet you, Naida. I hope Alice is all right?"

"Hullo, Mrs. Foxladle," Alice said as she came through the dividing door. "I've got your books behind the counter."

"Lovely!" She gave my hand another squeeze. "It was such a pleasure meeting you, dear."

I nodded, watching with a pathetic kind of longing as Alice pulled a stack of books from under the counter and proceeded to show them to the sweet older woman.

"I'm sorry it took so long to get these," she told Mrs. Foxladle. "My buyer has been ill."

I frowned. I was pretty sure Alice was buyer, owner, stockgirl, and spotted dick baker in one. So, why had she lied?

A few moments later, I waved goodbye as the elderly woman left and returned to my work.

"Thank you, dear," she said to someone at the door.

I glanced back up and saw her sliding past a young man with black hair and a cool gaze. He held the door for her and nodded when she thanked him again. Then he came inside the store.

I stood and gave him a welcoming smile. "Can I help you?" I asked.

He smiled shyly. "No, but thank you. I'm just going to look around."

"Of course. Just let me know if I can answer any questions." An unlikely possibility since I knew even less about the bookstore than I did about the artifact library, but I was getting pretty good at running to Alice for help.

He nodded and moved into the shelves, disappearing from view.

I squinted at my list of items to be cataloged. When Alice came back up front, I'd go finish that task. As much as I wanted to learn both parts of the business, I felt out of my element in the bookstore. Handling the artifacts made me happy. Even when I didn't understand them.

My phone rang. I looked at the ID and saw it was the realtor who was selling my grandma's home for me. I'd called her first thing that morning. "Hello?"

"Naida, hi. You left me a message?"

"Yes, I wanted to talk to you about the dispersal of the furnishings..."

A crash sounded down the stacks and I jumped. "Hold on." I stood up and went to the center aisle, peering toward the back. "Are you all right?"

Silence.

"Hello?"

The customer poked his dark head around the end of the farthest shelves. "Sorry, I dropped a book." He held up a thick tome covered in embossed leather. "The book and I are both fine."

I nodded, smiling, then returned to the front of the store and my conversation. "I'm back, sorry. Yes, I know we'd discussed selling all the furnishings with the house..."

Fifteen minutes later, my task complete, I disconnected and realized I hadn't heard any more from the customer. I headed toward the spot where I'd last seen him, intending to ask if he was doing okay.

I didn't find him in the expected aisle, or any other aisle for that matter. But I did notice something that made my eyes go wide.

I stood over a chalky circle on the carpet, frowning. Why would someone have drawn a circle on the carpet?

But worse, there was a slightly burnt smell hanging on the air. And a tinge of...rotten eggs?

My gaze slid to the framed picture lying face down on the rug. I walked over and picked it up. It was a picture of Alice with Fenwald clutched in her arms, standing in front of the Eiffel Tower.

A terrible but familiar stench wafted past, making my nose wrinkle with disgust. Those bangers were never going to go away.

My gaze slid to the wall where the picture had been hanging, and my fingers went numb.

The picture crashed back to the floor.

I took a step back. But I forced myself to stop. "Holy fish fingers!"

What I was seeing wasn't right. And I was pretty sure it was my job to look into it.

6

THAT SEALED IT...I'M DEFINITELY LOSING MY MIND

" A lice!!"

I stared at the whirling circular hole in the wall, the magic spinning velvet black with pink, purple and vivid orange streaks mixing in from the edges to meld at the center. The spinning vortex pulled on me, tugging me forward. My eyes were wide and unblinking, my peripheral vision filled with the same swirling magic reflected in my pupils. Before I even knew I'd moved, I was standing in front of it, one hand stretched toward the whirling, addictive energy.

Pain flashed through my mind, and I blinked as something thumped to the floor.

I looked down at the slender book of spells, entitled *Creative Spell work for Protection and Comfort*.

As I looked at it, the book flew back off the floor,

danced on the air in front of me as if giving me a piece of its mind, and then flew back to its spot on the shelves.

I swallowed hard.

"Okay..." That had been close. I reached out and slid a fingertip down the book's spine. "Thank you."

It hopped in its spot and settled back to inactivity.

"Alice!!" I yelled again. I didn't know what to do. I was afraid to leave the vortex unwatched long enough to go fetch the Keeper. But she wasn't responding to my shouts. Then I remembered she'd mumbled something about a nap earlier. There was no way she'd hear me all the way upstairs in her apartment.

I'd have to open the connecting door and shout up to her.

But something told me I needed to keep an eye on the vortex.

I backed slowly toward the door, through the narrow space between the ends of the shelving and the wall. My hand reaching blindly for the door handle, I found the knob and turned it, yanking the door open. I quickly stuck my head through and bellowed for Alice as loudly as I could.

A warm, furry form slipped past my legs and trotted toward the vortex, raggedy tail waving lazily behind him.

"Fenwald, no!" I hurried after him, terror making it hard to breathe. "Stop, you crazy cat! Don't go near that," I told him.

He stopped just in front of the vortex, dropping to his wide haunches and cocking his head as he examined it.

Some of my fear leached away. He wasn't getting too close. Maybe he had more sense than I thought...

Fenny turned and gave me a look. With narrowed gaze, he told me what he thought of my warning, "Yeow!" And then he leaped toward the hole, disappearing inside.

"No!" I dove at him and missed, hitting the carpet and skidding painfully over the empty spot where the big feline had been.

My knees and elbows stung with rug burn, and I'd bitten my tongue when I landed. I crawled painfully to my feet and stared at the hole. "Fenwald," I muttered, completely overcome.

Alice was going to kill me.

I sucked in a breath and forced myself to move closer to the whirling energy. It was flat against the surface of the wall, like an animated photo stuck to the plaster. I couldn't tell by looking at it that it was open. But I'd seen Fenwald fall into it, so I knew it wasn't what it seemed.

Taking another deep breath, I closed my eyes for a moment, tried to draw my Keeper magic around me, and then reached a hand toward the whirling energy. The energy grabbed my wrist and tugged hard, yanking me inside the terrifying whirlwind of magical energy.

Energy bit my skin like fire-ants, the sensation overpowering, swift, and terrible.

I had just enough time to panic at the idea that it might never let me go, and then it spit me out into a well-lit space with a concrete floor and lots of shelves. I hit the floor running and rammed almost immediately into a long table, covered in a jumble of items.

The artifact library.

"Ow!" I mumbled, whether in memory of the stinging bite of the vortex's magic or from my pubic bones slamming into the table, I wasn't sure.

Fenwald looked at me and meowed as if to say, "What took you so long?" He was sitting atop the table, seemingly unharmed.

I took a deep breath at the sight, relieved beyond words.

But something else was wrong.

I peered around the big cat. "Did Alice come and take that off the table?" I asked him, feeling silly for talking to a cat.

He turned and looked at the spot as if he'd understood my question, then pulled himself upright and batted a tiny piece of fluff to the floor with an enormous paw, jumping down after it.

So much for the secret genius of Fenwald.

I stared at the conspicuously empty spot on the table, frowning. The bumpy, stained suitcase was gone.

Why was it gone? Who'd taken it? I decided it had to be Alice, but I had no idea why she would have removed it from the table before I'd gotten it cataloged. And, if it was Alice, why had the vortex led me there?

The bell on Croakies' front door jangled softly. I panicked, realizing there was a magical vortex spinning on the wall and a human customer might have just come into the store.

That was not good.

I hurried toward the dividing door and burst into the bookstore, looking frantically around. "Hello?"

Nobody answered me.

Nothing seemed to be moving.

I ran down the center walkway, peering down every aisle.

Nobody.

My gaze slid to the spot where the vortex had been. I skidded to a stop at the end of the aisle.

It was gone.

The wall was smooth and unblemished. The picture of Alice and Fenwald in front of the Eiffel Tower was hanging back in its spot.

And I was apparently losing my mind.

Alice stood with her arms crossed over her chest and her chin jutting. Next to her, his tail sliding over the cool concrete floor, Fenwald jutted his chin too. Oliver, the tree frog, had no chin to jut, so he contented himself with blinking accusingly in my direction.

I bit back the chorus of excuses I'd been making to myself since learning the artifact library had been robbed, and I'd somehow missed the whole thing.

"Tell me again," Alice said in a tone filled with exaggerated patience. "How this happened right under your nose."

I bit my tongue against the desire to remind her that her pug nose had been in the same vicinity as mine. One could even argue it had been closer to the scene of the crime than mine had been.

"A man came into the store…"

"What did he look like?" Alice interrupted.

I opened my mouth to describe him and realized I couldn't. "I…don't remember."

Alice sighed, the sound like a martyr's last breath. "You didn't see him? I thought you were sitting right there in the bookstore."

"I was." I frowned as I remembered looking right at him. "I saw him. Even talked to him. But for some reason, I can't remember anything about him."

I'd expected another martyr's exhalation on that one, but Alice looked thoughtful instead. "Go on."

"I asked him if he needed help and he told me he just wanted to look around."

When I didn't continue, Alice sent me a sharp look, lifting a slightly bushy eyebrow.

"I heard a thump a few minutes later and called out to him. He popped his head out from between the aisles and told me he'd just dropped a book." My mind formed the picture of a dark head, the face a blur within a softly formed outline. "I went back to work until I realized I hadn't heard anything from him for a while. Then, I went looking and found the vortex."

"Describe the scene completely," Alice ordered.

I thought about it for a moment, wanting to get it right. My brain pulled together the details I could dredge up. Like the man's face, everything about the vortex and the area around it seemed suddenly muzzy.

"I remember a foul stench..." I said. My eyes went wide as I realized my mistake.

"Like sulfur?" Alice asked.

I shook my head, wrapping my arms protectively around myself. "No, it was probably nothing."

"No. Scent is key. Magical energy usually leaves behind a rotten-egg smell. Are you sure it wasn't like that?"

How did I tell her I was smelling her cooking?

"I...I thought maybe I was smelling spoiled meat." There, that didn't imply her cooking. Did it?

She arched both brows. "Spoiled meat?"

I nodded.

"Like what we smell here, now?"

I blinked. "What?" I realized my sense of smell had gone numb to that particular scent. But I thought about it and realized I had smelled it at the cataloging table first. "Yes. You're right. I smelled it here this morning. When you were coo..." I quickly swallowed the word, hoping she didn't catch my meaning.

I'm never that lucky.

"When I was cooking?" Alice's small eyes turned to hard little pebbles behind her oversized glasses. "You thought the stink was coming from my cooking?"

My mouth opened and snapped closed. Then it opened again. I gave her a sickly smile. "Sorry."

She shook her head. "Brilliant." Alice pulled her cell phone out of her pocket and dialed a number.

"Are you calling Detective Grym?" Despite my best efforts not to grimace, I felt my face forming into a frown anyway. The last thing I wanted was to face the dour detective with yet another failure proclaiming my inadequacy. In fact, I'd left his car the day before promising myself I'd avoid him at all costs in the future.

Alice stared at me as a ringing sound came

through the phone. Finally, a small voice said, "Hello?"

"Lea, sweetums, do you think you could pop over for a few minutes?"

Alice listened to the response and then nodded. "Brilliant. Cheers!" She hung up and gave me a cool glance. "Leandra is an earth witch. Hopefully, she'll be able to read the magic signature of our thief."

I liked the sound of that. But I would have equally appreciated the sound of being beaten about the head and shoulders with a pencil if it meant there'd be no Detective Dismal. "Good!" I started toward the front of the building, looking forward to seeing a real witch at work.

A shrill whistle sliced the silence and I jumped, skidding to a stop and turning.

Alice shook her head. "I'd like you to stay here and finish cataloging these items, please."

"But..."

She shook her head and headed past me. "If you'd finished the cataloging before you went gallivanting off, the thief wouldn't have had an opportunity to steal that artifact."

I stood there, fuming for several moments after the dividing door clicked shut behind her with an unnecessary thump.

It wasn't fair. None of it was fair. I only took up the cataloging to be useful and to learn about the artifacts quicker. And it hadn't been my idea to go hunting the missing killer shoes. It had been Alice's.

"Fermented fish farts!" I mumbled.

Then I turned on my heel and started back toward the table. Maybe if I hurried, I could get the rest of the artifacts cataloged before Lea arrived.

I knew that was an impossibility as the warning bell from the front door jangled happily through the library.

I sank into depression.

Nothing I did was right. Maybe my grandma had been right all those years when she repeatedly told me I wasn't cut out to be a magical person.

Clearly, I was dealing with some serious inadequacies in that department.

With a sigh, I trudged toward the table.

I didn't quite make it.

With a hop and a jaunty jig, Casanova's chair skidded across the room and scooped me up, taking off with a squeal of wooden legs on concrete. I grabbed hold of the arms to keep from being flung aside as it took me for a fast ride through the artifact library. The chair shot forward, then backward, then spun in dizzying circles, while invisible fingers pinched my imprisoned butt cheeks, making me jump and yelp in outrage even as I clung to the oversexed, fast-moving furniture.

As it reached the garage-sized door at the back, the chair spun in a tight turn and shot back toward the front at a speed that made my eyes water and my shoulder-length brown hair stream out behind me.

By that point, I was shrieking in terror, but the chair ignored me and moved even faster. Until it reached Shakespeare's desk near the front of the artifact library.

Without warning, it squealed to a stop, and I was propelled out of it.

I flew through the air, too terrified to do much more than throw my hands out to catch myself, and landed half-covering the big desk, hands splayed on the leather blotter at its center.

I was vaguely aware of the gnish of a chair spinning on its back legs and scurrying away before I could pull myself together and retaliate.

Beneath my palms, the blotter began to warm and roll, startling a short bark of surprise out of me and sending me scurrying away.

I watched, fascinated as energy spiked the air around the desk. Curious, I held out a hand and felt magic sliding over my skin.

Like butterfly wings on a warm summer day.

It wasn't an unpleasant feeling at all, and my heart slowly returned to normal as I watched the desk work its magic.

Being Shakespeare's desk, I fully expected a sheet of paper to appear proclaiming some wise and witty Shakespearianism. Instead, there was a sudden flash of bright light above the desk, and a sheet of paper appeared, hanging in midair. The page had words carefully printed across its surface in a heavy, dark hand.

Beware the implements of travel, for they oft be deadly.

Okay, that sealed it. I was definitely losing my mind.

7

WHOOO?

I stood back and tried to make myself invisible. Alice was mad at me, and I was afraid she would make me go in the back if she thought I too interested in what Lea was doing.

But I *was* interested. Too interested to want to be banished.

I wielded the dusting feather with careless abandon, not paying any attention to what I was dusting. I was pretty sure there were two or three books that were as pristine as the day they'd come off the presses, and the rest could be buried in dust for all I knew.

My attention was intensely focused elsewhere.

Lea had laid out a circle beyond the one that was on the carpet. That circle had gotten smudged from somebody's shoes...I'm not digging too deeply into that one...and a winding path of cat paws.

She'd placed a thick white candle in the center on a small round mirror and surrounded it on four sides with smaller candles. Then she'd placed a wide, shallow bowl containing a pile of pale green leaves in the middle of the original circle.

"What's that?" Alice asked.

I leaned closer as Lea twisted, pulling a fireplace lighter from her bag. "Wormwood."

"Ah." Alice nodded. "To enhance divination."

Lea lit the leaves and straightened. In one hand, she held a bundle of sticks wrapped in what looked like parchment paper and a piece of chalk. As I watched, she dipped a feather quill in a tiny bottle of some kind of red ink and wrote across the paper with it.

"What's in the paper?" I asked before I could stop myself.

Alice's gaze shot to me, and her face tightened.

I gave her a look that I hoped showed I wasn't going to back down. Despite what she seemed to think, I was pretty sure the loss of the suitcase artifact wasn't my fault.

Mostly sure.

"Licorice Root," Lea said. "It should give me some control over the shadow of the intruder once it arrives."

I felt my eyes go wide. That didn't sound terrifying at all.

No, it did not.

"Is that blood?" Alice asked, nodding toward the small bottle of ink.

Lea shook her head. "I don't dabble in blood magics. It's *Synsepalum dulcificum*, otherwise known as magic berry or redberry. It's a transformative medium, enforcing the magics of the other herbs."

I gave up pretending to dust and found myself moving closer.

Lea looked at Alice. "You should step back. I don't want you to get stung when the circle engages."

Alice backed down the aisle and stopped next to me.

Lea knelt inside her circle and bent over the largest candle first. As she lit it, she muttered, "*Ostende mihi*," then waited until the wick grabbed the flame before moving around the circle. With each lighting of the remaining candles, she repeated the original phrase, "*Ostende mihi.*"

The flame of the center candle shot twelve inches into the air and sizzled with energy. The flame spluttered orange with bursts of green in the center candle and the color of blood in the other four candles.

As she lit the final candle, Lea stood and lifted her hands, her chanting too soft for me to make out the words. Though, I suspected I wouldn't have understood them anyway since they were in Latin, and I'd all but failed my Latin classes in school.

As Lea chanted, pale green energy rose from the

floor inside the circle and lifted toward the ceiling, filling the magical cylinder she'd created with her circle.

She stood at the center of the magic and used the parchment wrapped Licorice Root to fan the smoke coming from the bowl in the center.

Smoke rose from the bowl and thickened, spinning into a charcoal gray column that spread outward and took shape.

A denser part at the top formed into wide shoulders and sprouted a shape from its center that coalesced into a head. The torso narrowed to a waist, bumped slightly out into hips, and broke into two columns that became legs.

The smoke was shaped like a man.

I grabbed Alice's arm. "That looks like the guy who was in here before the vortex showed up."

Alice nodded.

We watched as the smoke-man turned to look at Lea, who was still chanting softly. Still waving the parchment-wrapped bundle in his direction.

Smoky hands found blurry-edged hips. He seemed to be glaring at her, determined not to obey the dictates of her magic.

But Lea lifted the parchment to her mouth and blew softly on it. The effect was immediate. The smoky shape was blown toward the wall where the vortex had been. As it touched the drywall, the picture hanging there disappeared, along with the drywall behind it, and the vortex reappeared.

Smoke-man blew through the vortex. To my shock, Lea didn't hesitate. She stepped closer and then followed him in.

Alice and I looked at each other, wondering what we should do. Finally, we turned and ran toward the connecting door, threw it open, and ran into the library.

There was no sign of Lea or smoke man.

"Where'd they go?" I asked.

Alice opened her mouth to say something but never got the chance.

A thunderous roar and a whoosh exploded from the bookstore. We ran back to the front, arriving just in time to see a column of flame blast toward the ceiling, flare violently, and then dribble down Lea's magic cylinder like water sliding down the sides of a glass tube.

Too late to catch her, we watched Lea collapse bonelessly onto the carpet.

Her clothes were actually smoking. And her skin was blistered and red as if she'd been burned. She was lying in a crumpled heap on the floor inside the circle she'd drawn. The chalk edge was smudged where her hand lay upon it. She had chalk on one fingertip, leading me to think she'd smudged it on purpose.

"Where'd she come from?" I asked Alice as the Keeper ran over and knelt down beside Lea.

Alice ignored my question and reached for the witch, her hand snapping back as if she'd been burned by the contact. Holding her hand against her chest, Alice lifted a haunted gaze to me. "I need to call the doctor."

My eyes went wide. "A regular human doctor? Is that a good idea?"

Alice pulled a phone from her pocket. "Don't be daft." She punched a number and, a beat later, spoke into the phone. "I need your help."

As Alice disconnected, Lea groaned. Her fingers twitched as she came awake.

"Don't move, sweetums," Alice crooned. "Doctor Whom's on his way."

I blinked. "You called Doctor Who?" Okay, that was just too crazy, even for Croakies.

"Whom," Alice corrected me. Her gaze jerked up as a breezy whoosh filled the room, followed by a soft thump. "Your human is showing," she said, smiling gently. "Over here!" she called out.

I stood as a man hurried around the shelves, my gaze widening with surprise at the sight.

He looked to be about five feet tall. Maybe less. His form was pear-shaped only more...sloped. He wore a cloak of feathers that drooped from narrow shoulders and covered wide hips over short, skinny legs. His bowed calves were covered in fitted, yellow socks, making them look too much like bird legs, and his feet were bare, the toes long and curved downward like claws.

Tugging a stethoscope out from under the feathered cloak, the doc blinked slowly at me through enormous eyes, which were set close together on either side of a sharp, beaklike nose. His lips pursed as his owlish gaze settled onto Lea. "Whooo?"

"The earth witch from next door," Alice said, moving away from Lea so the doctor could come closer.

He didn't so much crouch beside Lea as...nest... there, placing the scope on the curve of her throat and then at her temple.

"Um..." I started to say, but I was shushed by Alice. My lips slammed shut.

Doctor Whom sliced a curved finger claw into the skin of Lea's wrist, and I stepped forward. "Hey!"

Alice glared at me. "Be still!"

Frowning, I crossed my arms over my chest, watching as blood beaded along the scratch he'd made.

Whom lifted the blood-covered claw toward his nose and sniffed. Then he turned away and hawked several times, regurgitating a small bundle of bones and fur that landed on the carpet beside him.

"Ew!" I objected loudly.

Alice rolled her eyes. "Watch and learn."

The good doctor scooped the contents of his

stomach from the rug and carefully packed it over the slice he'd made in Lea's arm. Then he settled down with his back to us and began whistling softly.

Nothing happened for long minutes. I started to get restless, moving from foot to foot and trying to see beyond the doctor's feathery bulk to Lea. "Maybe we should take her to the hospital," I whispered to Alice.

Whom's head turned nearly backward to glare at me. "Patience, young woman." He frowned, glancing at Alice. "Whooo?"

"My apprentice," she admitted, seemingly without joy.

I bristled. "Look, I'm getting tired..."

Whom whistled again.

My gaze slid past him, to the substance rising from Lea's arm. I watched in fascination as oily black smoke saturated the ball of stuff the Doc had plastered over Lea's wound. When the smoke stopped wafting out and the last of it had settled into the "poultice" Doctor Whom had put in place, the Doc reached over and gathered the blackened goop with his claws, flinging it over his shoulder. It dissipated on the air with a soft pop of sound.

Lea sighed and her eyes came open.

She looked from Whom to us and then back to the doctor. "That bad, huh?"

Whom laughed. "A minor hex poisoning. Nothing we couldn't nip right in the bud." He unfolded himself from the nesting position and dropped the stethoscope back around his neck. The doc pulled a pad of paper from a pocket and scribbled on it, tearing off a sheet and handing it to Lea. "Your bill for my services," he said. Then he reached into a different pocket and tugged out a small rodent, holding it by the tail. It wriggled in terror, its little paws beating the air. "One mouse a day for a week. Here's your first dose."

Lea reached out and took the frightened critter, rubbing a soothing finger along its trembling body. "Thanks, Doc."

He spun his head all the way around and smiled. "Pleasure. Good day to you all."

The rotund little owl-man waddled around the shelves and I hurried after him, fascinated to know how he'd gotten to us so quickly.

An oversized wooden birdhouse squatted in the center of the open space at the front of the store. One wall of the small building rested against the table where I'd been working on my notes. The doctor's conveyance had lifted the table a few inches off the floor on one side, dumping several sheets of paper to the carpet.

I made a small sound of delight at the sight. He opened the door of the charming structure, and several more mice ran out, escaping to relative safety underneath the bookshelves.

"That should cover the rest of the week," he

called over his shoulder. And then he disappeared inside, slamming the door firmly closed.

A beat later lights emanated from the windows of the small building. Doctor Whom's birdhouse lifted off the carpet, spun several times, and disappeared with a whoosh.

"Holy owl spit!" I said, grinning widely. "That was icy."

Lea came up and stood beside me, still holding the tiny mouse. It fixed me with a shiny black gaze, and I reached out to stroke a finger over its tiny white head. "You're not really going to ea..."

Lea covered my mouth with her hand. "Shhh! You'll scare the little guy. Of course not. None of us follow Whom's after-treatment orders. We just take our 'medicine' so he doesn't eat it."

The little mouse gave off an alarmed shriek and Lea blanched. "Oh. Sorry." She settled the creature to the floor. "Off with you now. Find your friends."

Alice sighed. "I'll have to have a talk with Fenwald. He's quite the hunter, you know."

Our gazes slid toward the front windowsill, where said *hunter* was licking his nether regions in the sun, oblivious to the newly arrived rodent family mere feet from his nose.

I snickered.

Lea had better sense. She cleared her throat. "Okay, so that was interesting. Whoever that was, he did go directly to the table and take the suitcase.

Before he picked it up, he held a palm over it, and the thing jumped around as if he was drawing something from it."

I felt my eyes go wide. "You think there was something alive in there?"

Lea seemed to consider that for a moment, then she shook her head. "Something that had been magically attached, but not necessarily alive."

"Magically attached?" I asked.

"She means the suitcase was under the power of something. Or someone," Alice clarified. She narrowed her gaze on Lea. "You suspect a mage?"

"Specifically a wizard," Lea agreed. "He probably attached a masking spell to the suitcase so you couldn't read any negative energy from it. That all but ensured you wouldn't lock it into the toxic magic vault."

Alice curled her lip.

"What?" I asked, only about half understanding their conversation.

"Wizards are nasty," Lea said.

"How'd he get back out with the artifact?" Alice asked the witch.

Lea sighed. "I can't be entirely sure." She raised her gaze to ours. "He..." She bit her lip. "After he lifted the suitcase, he turned around and..." She shook her head, clearly struggling with what she needed to tell us.

"What is it?" Alice asked, impatience in her tone.

"He saw me. He shouldn't have been able to see me. He was only a shadow. Something that happened in the past. But the shadow turned and saw me and..." Her gaze turned haunted. She shuddered violently and rubbed her arms, hugging herself.

"What is it?" I asked. "What happened in there, Lea?"

The earth witch expelled air in a rush, looking thoroughly spooked. "He threw a hex at me and I flew out of the divining. He cast me out of something that happened in the past. I didn't even know that was possible. We're dealing with a deadly and powerful wizard."

8

THIS IS YOUR LEGACY MAGIC

"Could you tell what he looked like?" I asked the witch.

Lea shook her head. "It doesn't work like that. What we were looking at was simply a shadow of what happened." She rubbed her arms as if chilled. "There shouldn't have been any crossover between the past and the present."

"Except there was," Alice offered.

"Yes." Lea sighed. "I need to run some tests. Do you mind if I hang out here for a while?"

"That's fine, sweetums." Alice glanced at me. "We'll just get back to work." She all but danced toward the closet beside the tea counter, pulling out a coat and slipping it on. "I'm going to retrieve an artifact," she happily told the room at large.

Excitement filling me, I hurried over. "I'll get my stuff."

"Don't bother. You can't come with." Alice said it with such glee, it took me a moment to grasp that she was shutting me down.

"What? But why? I need to learn..."

"Because I can't close the shop, so you'll stay here in case customers come in."

I bit down on the urge to ask her why she couldn't close it. She'd likely done it countless times before I'd come around. But part of me wanted to stay and watch Lea work without Alice around to interfere. That sounded almost as good as going artifact hunting. "Will I be able to go with you soon? I need to learn."

"Of course, sweetums. You have a lot to learn. And much of it is here." She patted my hand, giving me a smile that almost looked sincere. "Detective Grym was right. I pushed you too hard before. I'm going to give you some time to learn the ropes in the store before we move on to the next thing."

That sounded reasonable, so I nodded. "Okay."

Alice headed for the door. "I'll bring dinner back." She grinned. "Tacos?"

The day was looking up. "That sounds great."

I watched her leave and then started toward Lea, intending to ask her a lot of questions. Unfortunately, it wasn't meant to be.

The front doorbell jangled and I looked over to find two women coming into the store, chatting and laughing happily.

Customers.

Barely biting back a sigh, I headed in their direction.

I'd never seen the shop so busy. Of course, I'd only really spent time there for the last two days. But hardly anyone had come into the store the day before.

An hour later, Lea came around the end of the shelves with her small magic bag. She looked tired. "I'm done for now. I'll get back to you with the results of my tests."

I nodded. "Do you want some tea? You look done in."

She smiled, "Thanks. That would be nice."

Lea sat at the table with my newly stacked notes, and stared into space as if she were utterly drained. A few minutes later, I settled tea and a plate of cookies on the table and joined her there. "I'm tired too," I told her. "It wasn't nearly this busy yesterday."

Lea sipped her tea, a knowing spark in her turquoise gaze.

I raised a brow. "What?"

She laughed softly. "I've known Alice for three years now. I can't remember her ever wrangling an artifact on a Monday. It's her busiest day."

I read between the lines for what Lea didn't say.

"That's why she left me here. She saw an opportunity to escape a hard day's work and took it."

Lea grinned around her cookie, which was fortunately something Alice purchased at the local bakery instead of making it herself. As evidenced by the fact that we both still had our teeth.

"That rat," I murmured, sighing.

"At least you're getting dinner out of it."

I laughed. "She is right, though. I do need to learn this part of the business. The magic stuff will come soon enough."

Something in the way I said it made Lea tip her head. "You're not comfortable with the magic?"

I held her gaze for a long moment, wondering if I dared confide my doubts to her. After a moment, I decided Lea was trustworthy. "I'll be honest, I don't know what I'm doing...magically speaking. I was never formally trained. My ability has pretty much consisted of getting bad headaches and drawing random floating objects."

Lea's expression tightened, and I immediately regretted telling her. I'd been afraid of exactly that reaction. The reaction of a seasoned magic user when faced with a clumsy novice. I didn't ask her what the face was about. I just started to climb to my feet. "Well, I guess I should get back to work..."

Lea's hand came out and clasped mine. "If you ever need advice..." She hesitated as if unsure whether her offer would be welcome. Then she smiled. "I'm just next door."

My surprise must have shown because she gave my hand a squeeze. "We've all been there, Naida."

I collapsed back into my chair. "I doubt you were ever where I am. I'm terrified Alice will figure out I'm a fraud." As soon as the words slid past my lips, I panicked. My head shot up and I covered my mouth. "You won't tell her?"

Lea stared at me for a long moment. Then she reached out with both hands, palms facing me, and waved them in front of my face, about six inches away.

I blinked in surprise. "What are you doing?"

She let her hands drop. "Your aura is purple, did you know that?"

"Um…"

"Sorcerers generally have auras that are anywhere from lilac to deep purple. The depth of the color informs the level of power you possess."

"But I'm not a sorcerer," I objected.

Lea picked up her tea. "Your power ranges in the upper third. Not the deepest purple, but certainly not lilac."

"What are you telling me?" My voice was breathless. I was suddenly terrified to fail her assessment.

"I'm telling you that you come from a powerful line of sorcerers. Even untrained, your magical aura is strong. I suspect you will only grow in strength with training." She grimaced. "I'd bet my favorite hex that Alice knows you're strong, and her treatment of you is probably based on a mix of jealousy and the knowledge that you can take care of yourself, despite her inadequate training."

I thought about that, not really believing it. "I wish that were true."

"I assure you it is. I can see it."

I leaned over the table. "But I've been told I'm not magical."

"If that's true, then why are you here?"

I shrugged. "Someone thought I might like it."

I expected her to ask who that someone was, but she didn't. Instead she asked, "Why did they think that?"

I chewed my lip for a beat before I told her. "Things started...following me...when I turned eighteen."

"Following you?"

"Yes. It's hard to explain."

Lea's face took on a strange look and she slowly smiled, nodding to something over my shoulder. "You mean like that?"

I jerked my head around and sucked air in surprise. Reaching up, I quickly snatched the slim volume of magical spells from the air where it hovered. I looked around to make sure there were no customers in the area. "That's been happening more since I came to Croakies."

"The magic is drawn to your energy, Naida," Lea told me gently. "The only thing you need in order to succeed is for you to embrace your own power."

"What are you telling me?" I asked, my mind reluctant to grasp her meaning.

"I'm telling you that you *are* magical, Naida. You're actually a strong sorceress. And that, however you came to be at Croakies, you're in the right place."

She leaned closer and smiled. "You were born to be a Keeper of the Artifacts. This is your legacy magic. And I predict that you're going to be very good at it once you accept the magic your heredity has given you."

I stared at the book of spells, wondering why anyone would want to perform spells to make bunions appear on someone's feet. "I hope you're right."

Lea stood up. "I'm not only right..." She plucked her bag off the spare chair. "I think you know that what I'm saying is true." She headed for the door. "Why don't you stop by the shop tomorrow afternoon? We'll have tea."

"I'd love that."

"Good." She pulled the door open, setting the bell to jangling. "I'm looking forward to chatting some more."

A man in a green uniform held the door for Lea and then came into the bookstore as she left. He was holding a metal clipboard with a thick sheaf of papers clipped to its surface. He looked at the top sheet and then at me. "Naida Griffith?"

I read the emblem embroidered on the pocket of his shirt. GMM, which I knew stood for Glasswart's Magical Movers. I knew that because I'd called them. "I'm Naida Griffith," I told him, eagerly.

He handed me the clipboard. "I just need you to sign on the bottom to accept delivery."

Using the pen he'd clipped to the board, I signed my name across the top sheet.

"Where would you like your stuff?" he asked.

"Actually, if you could pull around to the back, there's a bigger door. I'd like you to bring it through there."

"We can certainly do that."

I grinned widely. "Awesome sauce! I'll meet you back there."

9

I'LL BE DARNED LIKE THE GODDESS'S
FAVORITE SOCKS

I settled the last pillow into place and grinned. The spot I'd chosen was deep inside the artifact library, in a shadowed corner beneath a high window that allowed a narrow beam of sunlight to paint the colorful rag rug at the center of the space.

Along with the rug, I'd brought my twin-sized bed, one dresser, and my grandma's favorite recliner for reading, as well as splurging on the television from Grandma's sitting room. I'd placed the TV on an old trunk that had once belonged to my mother, according to Grandma Neely. I'd sifted through the stuff inside the trunk after Grandma had died, finding nothing more interesting than a couple of hand-knitted throws, a mirror and brush set, and a yellowed white porcelain teapot, which was chipped in a couple of spots.

I left everything except the throws in the trunk and asked the GMM guys to place the television on it. Eying the antenna Grandma had used to avoid paying for cable or satellite services, I decided I might be able to set it on top of one of the shelves with a direct line of sight to a window.

That should work well enough to get me the shows I liked.

It wasn't a lovely spot. But it was cozy. And, filled with my own stuff, it felt like home.

The bookstore bell jangled, the sound a soft chime that somehow filled the entire library space. Rubbing my hands over my dusty jeans, I hurried back to the front. It had to be Alice returning from her artifact wrangling. I'd locked the door to customers an hour earlier.

My stomach rumbled as I thought of the promised tacos, and the thought made me walk faster.

Throwing the dividing door open, I found Alice standing in the opening of the front door, listening to a certain grim-faced detective on the sidewalk. Pun intended.

"...body was dumped in Enchanted Park."

My ears perked at that little bit of partial information. "What body?" I asked.

Alice turned with a scowl, though her eyes looked more worried than mad. "Don't worry, Naida.

It has nothing to do with us," she told me in a firm voice.

I couldn't help wondering if Alice was trying to convince me, or the eagle-eyed detective on the sidewalk.

"Can I come inside?" Grym asked, his gaze sliding to mine.

I nodded, even as Alice shook her head. "Sorry, we're closed for the night. I've told you all I know."

Grym's jaw tightened. "Would you rather I return with a search warrant?"

"For what?" Alice asked, shoving her ugly square glasses up her short nose.

"For being generally uncooperative," Grym responded, his jaw tightening with irritation. His expression was murderous, and he was leaning aggressively forward as if he was considering giving her a pop on the pug nose.

I could appreciate his apparent desire to pummel Alice about the head and shoulders. Goddess knew I'd been there a few times already in my extremely short tenure at Croakies. But I didn't think a rage-induced pummeling would be in anybody's best interests. "Would you like some tea, Detective?" I asked, determinedly avoiding Alice's gaze.

"That would be nice," he said through gritted teeth.

Alice finally turned and stomped away from the door. "I'll make it."

I indicated the nearby table. "Please, have a seat. What's going on, Detective Grym?"

He sat, crossing one leg over the other at the ankle, and expelled a weary breath. "I'm afraid we've found the body of a man not too far from here."

I frowned. "Do you know who it is?"

He shook his dark head, his gaze sliding to Alice and taking on a speculative glint. "No. Only that he's not human. He's a gnome."

Alice's narrow shoulders stiffened as she poured hot water into a mug.

"A gnome?" I didn't want to tell the detective that I hadn't even known such creatures existed, so I asked another question. "What did he die of?"

His speculative glance slid in my direction. "He was murdered."

I hadn't been expecting that. "Yikes!"

Alice settled a steaming mug in front of Detective Grym and crossed her arms. Apparently, she and I weren't having tea. I bit back a sigh.

"My feelings exactly." Grym said, sipping his tea. "The victim was last seen here. At Croakies."

I glanced toward Alice. She flinched, her lips pinching tightly together. "I told you, Detective, I barely knew Gido. He came to offer security services, and I told him no. He left. End of story."

Grym sipped tea as silence throbbed through the room.

Having zero impulse control when it comes to

filling an uncomfortable silence, I attempted to fill it after what felt like an excruciatingly long moment. "If he was walking the neighborhood trying to sell his services, he must have visited several shops along this street," I offered helpfully.

Grym nodded. "He certainly did. From the small grocer to the travel agent. I've spoken to just about all of them. The problem is, I have several witnesses who insist they saw Alice and Gido arguing in front of Croakies." His gaze narrowed. "A few of them also reported seeing Alice smack him in the head with a broom."

Alice suddenly found her fingernails very interesting. I winced when I looked at them. I had the sudden thought that she should have found them interesting a few weeks earlier. They were a dry, ragged, and unadorned mess. "It was just a slight disagreement," she finally said.

"Slight?" Grym said, his voice dripping with warning. "You knocked him out."

Alice shrugged. "Who knew gnome's heads were so delicate. I figured it was made of concrete or something."

Alice gave up staring at her long-neglected fingernails and crossed her arms. "I can assure you that he walked away under his own steam as soon as he woke up."

"You're sure about that?" Grym asked.

"I am. I watched him leave."

"And exactly where were you when he scraped himself up off the sidewalk and left?" the detective demanded with a wry lift of an eyebrow.

Alice didn't hesitate. She pointed to the large window at the front of the store. "Standing right there in the window."

Grym jotted notes in a small notebook as she talked. "Which direction did he go when he left?" he asked.

"South," Alice said, pointing in the direction that led to downtown Enchanted.

"Did he get into a car?"

She shrugged. "Not within a couple of blocks. After I saw that he wasn't going to bother any more of my neighbors, I left him to himself."

Grym's dark-caramel gaze filled with suspicion. "Why did you fight with the gnome, Ms. Parker?"

She tapped one foot on the ground, her jaw jutting in a way that made her look downright pugnacious. For a long moment, I thought she wasn't going to answer. But she finally sighed, her jaw losing some of its mulish slant. "Are you familiar with Gnomish Security Services?" she asked the detective.

Grym lifted his chin, choosing not to respond.

She nodded, apparently taking that as verification. "Then you know why. Gido wasn't selling protection from an unlucky happenstance. He was offering me a chance not to get shaken down by

Gnomish itself. It's a protection racket, Detective. You know that and I know it. I was just letting him know that he wasn't going to get any business on this street. This is my berg, Detective Grym. And I'm not letting it be subjugated to a violent element."

Well, I'll be darned like the goddess's favorite socks. "Seriously? That stuff doesn't just happen on TV?" I asked, appalled.

Alice skimmed me a look. "I'm being perfectly serious. They start out asking you to pay a reasonable fee for their services. Then someone in the neighborhood gets robbed. Then a couple more. And suddenly everybody is paying a lot more for services they can't cancel under a not-so-veiled threat from Gnomish." She shook her head. "I've lived in a neighborhood that was 'protected' by those thugs once. I'm not doing it again."

Grym sighed. "You're not wrong. The Enchanted PD has been trying to catch them in an active case of defrauding customers, but they're good and they're careful." He eyed Alice carefully. "But none of that makes it okay to take the law into your own hands," he told Alice.

She held his gaze, not backing down. I respected that about her. "I give you my word that Gido got up and walked away under his own steam. I would have liked to do worse to him," she said. "But I didn't."

Grym stood up and headed for the door. "I might

need to ask you some more questions," he told Alice as he opened it. "Don't leave Enchanted."

We watched in silence as he left, closing the door quietly behind him. Alice hurried over and locked the door, flipping the sign to *Closed*.

She started pacing back and forth in the open space in front of the door. I watched her pace for a long moment, wondering if I was looking at the panic of a woman guilty of murder. I didn't think Alice was capable of such a thing. But then I'd only known her a couple of days. Not long enough to really know her at all.

I stood up, intending to say goodnight and flee back to my cozy little nook in the artifact library.

Unfortunately, my movement caught Alice's eye. Her head jerked around and her small eyes behind the enormous glasses locked onto me. "We need to figure out what happened to Gido."

I blinked in surprise. Of all the things I'd thought she might say, that hadn't been on the list. "Excuse me?"

She wrung her hands and started pacing again. "It's my only chance."

Ice slipped along my spine, making me shiver. "What do you mean, Alice? If you didn't kill him..."

Her head whipped around, her expression a mix of panic and anger. "I didn't kill anybody!"

Gilded gopher garters, the woman was a titch high strung. I lifted my hands. "I wasn't suggesting you had. I was just going to say that, if you didn't kill him you have nothing to worry about, right?"

Alice expelled a harsh breath. "Wrong. Oh, so wrong." She stopped in front of me, grabbing my hands in a painful grip. "I didn't kill him. But Gnomish is going to think I did. Which means we're in danger from them…"

The icy fear spread through my organs, turning me into a Naida-shaped popsicle from the inside out. "We?" I squeaked. "Why am I in danger?"

"You don't think they're going to just leave a witness behind when they murder me and slice me up into a thousand tiny pieces, do you?"

I grimaced at the gory visual. "Ugh!"

Alice nodded as if pleased that I'd finally grasped the situation in all of its ugly entirety. "Grym is going to keep digging into this, and he's going to find out…" She stopped suddenly, blinking rapidly, and then turned away from me and returned to pacing.

"Find out what?" I asked, my gaze narrowing.

"Nothing. We need to come up with a plan for figuring out how Gido was killed."

I dropped back into the chair I'd been trying to vacate. I didn't say anything because there was nothing I *could* say. If I'd thought I was untrained to be a KoA, I was triple that amount untrained to solve a murder. Then I had a thought. "Do you want me to work with Detective Grym…"

"No!" Alice screamed, slicing my question off like a hot knife through melted butter. "He's going to pin this on me if he can. We need to find the killer and hand him to the detective. It's the only way."

I didn't share her suspicion that Grym was incompetent. In fact, I believed he was really sharp. But she'd known him longer than I had. Maybe I was wrong. "I don't know how to investigate a murder," I told her.

She blew air through her lips, flapping a dismissive hand in my direction. "How hard can it be?"

I thought of Lea almost dying when we'd tried to discover how one large artifact had been taken out of the shop from under our noses. "Hard," I said.

"Are you telling me you won't even try?" Alice put her hands on her hips and glared at me.

I embraced a sudden wish that I'd been a bit faster in my escape. All I wanted to do was play with magical artifacts. It had never occurred to me that we'd be dealing with killers and deadly hexes. I took a deep breath and expelled it, shaking my head. "I'm telling you that I don't know how much assistance I'm going to be. But I'll be happy to help in any way I can."

That seemed to calm Alice down, which in turn calmed me down. "Good. That's good. Thanks, swee-tums." She headed toward the tea counter and I relaxed, thinking we were finally going to have our tea. But she walked past it to the closet. "Get your things. We're going out."

Even better! "Where are we going?"

Alice's smile was brittle and a bit scary. "To the scene of the crime. We're going to figure out *how* Gido was killed before that detective throws me in jail."

10

WHAT A GNISH

We stood at the edge of a small park in the middle of *Arcane Avenue*, four blocks up from Croakies. Yellow crime scene tape was wrapped around a spot that was about ten by twenty yards, which started at the sidewalk and stretched to a spot about three feet from the play structure at the center of the small park.

The grass inside the tape was well-trampled, but one area, in particular, was mashed beyond mere footsteps. From where we stood, it appeared to be a rectangular spot, about three feet long and two feet wide. "We need to get closer," Alice said, shoving her glasses up her nose.

Oliver, the tree frog, sat on her shoulder, peering hopefully at the nearby trees. I'd never seen him outside of Alice's ratty nest of brown hair, and wondered if the colorful little frog would make a hop for it if he saw an opening.

"Meow," Fenwick informed us from his location near our feet.

Alice gave him a speculative look. "Hmm...I wonder..."

"Ma'am, you need to keep that animal outside the tape."

I could almost hear Alice's thought processes grinding to a halt. She looked up and threw a vacant smile at the young Enchanted cop standing near the play structure. I hadn't noticed him when we arrived at the scene. But he was definitely there now.

As Fenwald batted at the yellow tape, the young cop put his hand on the butt of his gun. "I'll shoot him if he steps one paw on that grass."

The small crowd around us, who were also busily staring at the scene of the crime, gasped with outrage at his threat.

Despite the intimidating glare on his young face, I highly doubted the cop would shoot Fenwald. The public outcry would be more than the police would want to deal with just to protect a crime scene they'd probably already processed.

But, just in case, I reached down and scooped up the massive feline, groaning under his prodigious weight. "I think Fenny needs a diet," I told Alice.

She didn't seem to hear me. Her gaze had locked

onto the tree a couple of feet from where we stood. "I could send Oliver up..."

I blinked. "Can you see what he sees?" I asked, my eyes going wide. The whole magical thing was just too cool. And fraught with so many icy possibilities.

"Don't be silly," Alice told me, rolling her eyes. "He'd have to *tell* me what he saw." She frowned. "But frogs don't interpret things like we do. I doubt Olly would tell us what we need to know." She crossed her arms over her chest. "Bother."

I thought about how a frog might see the scene we were scrutinizing. He'd probably give her the fly and spider report.

"You're the Keeper, aren't you? From Croakies?"

Alice and I turned to find a woman about my height and age, with waist-length fire-red hair which she wore in two braids, gorgeous green eyes that shimmered with magic, and a full crop of freckles that painted her long, thin face and spilled down her throat into the high, straight neckline of her bright orange dress. The dress had long sleeves that covered her freckled hands in wide bells of fabric and fell below the knees of two skinny legs encased in green and white striped socks. The socks fit her like support stockings, emphasizing the skinniness of her legs, and were tall enough to disappear beneath the hem of the dress.

The puffy red coat she'd thrown on over the

costume didn't do much to make it more presentable.

"I'm the KoA," Alice said, her tone disinterested as she continued to peruse the taped-off area.

The creature's eyes flashed, turning even brighter than before, and she nodded. "I heard you were trying to stop Gnomish. I wanted to thank you. Somebody had to take them on."

Alice blinked in apparent surprise, "Oh. Well. It had to be done."

"Yes. And now I understand the cops are trying to pin Gido's death on you?"

"Unfortunately," Alice agreed on an airy sigh.

"I wanted to offer my help. If you need it."

Alice stared at the other woman for a moment, her beady eyes widening with recognition. "You live above the vapery."

"Yes. I'm Sebille."

"I know who you are!" Alice said a bit too loudly. Then she frowned. "You're kind of large for a sprite, aren't you?"

The red-haired woman lowered her fiery brows in pique.

Alice moved closer and lowered her voice. "I've heard about you. You're not just any sprite. Your mother is the qu…"

The woman turned abruptly away. "Please let me know if I can be of assistance."

"Wait!" Alice called out, halting the woman mid-step. "I could use your help right now if you wouldn't mind."

Sebille turned sharply on her heel and stalked back to us. "What?"

"Do you think you could make like a bug and check out that crime scene area for me? I'm trying to find the real killer, so the police will stop pestering me."

Sebille turned her startling gaze on me. It was a look that seemed to say, "And who are you?"

I wiggled my fingers at her. "Hi. I'm Naida. Keeper to Be."

Her eyes went wide. "You're in training?"

"I am." I bit my bottom lip to keep from making lots of excuses for my ineptitude. After all, I was pretty sure nobody knew about that but me, Alice, and maybe Detective Grym. Oh, and Lea. I sighed. "It's been a very...active two days."

The green eyes flashed. To my surprise, she grinned. "You've been in training for two days and you're already embroiled in a murder investigation?" She laughed as if I'd given her the best news she'd had all day. "What a gnish."

I frowned. "Hey!" I would have defended myself, but there was also the whole vortex thing. I was starting to think I was cursed. "Surely, it's not normal for this Keeper gig to be so...interesting." I told her.

The air in front of me started to swirl and shimmer. A tiny, crabby face appeared out of nowhere, and I yelped in surprise. The rest of the small body materialized in a flash of light that had me taking several steps back until my calves bumped up against the yellow tape.

The creature that had suddenly popped into existence in front of me was about four inches tall and had drab, brown wings that beat the air in an annoyed rhythm behind her. Her small head was covered in tight, dirty-blonde pin curls, and as she looked at me she arched a pair of very judgmental eyebrows. "Why did you call me?"

Sebille rolled her eyes and reached out with a long, skinny finger. "Nobody called you, Shirley." She poked the minuscule creature in the belly, causing her to grunt in outrage. The tiny wings beat the air with renewed violence. Shirley glared in my direction. "Don't ever call me again!" Then she disappeared in another flash of light, leaving behind a wisp of sulfur-scented air.

I gave the sprite a confused look.

Sebille shrugged. "That was Shirley. She's a pixie and she doesn't like to be called." As if that explained everything, Sebille transferred her attention to Alice. "What kinds of things are you looking for?"

I barely listened to Alice's response as I stared at the spot where the pixie had disappeared. Shirley? But I hadn't called... Then I realized what I'd done and laughed, drawing a question in the form of an arched, fire-red eyebrow from Sebille.

I just shook my head.

"So, will you help?" Alice asked

"I'll help you," the sprite said, looking directly at me.

I realized she'd deliberately cut Alice out of that message and couldn't help wondering why. She was clearly annoyed at the Keeper over something.

Feeling the need to respond in some way, I gave her a nod. "Thanks."

The sprite popped away in a flash of light, leaving me squinting at the spot where she'd been. Fenwald leaped off the ground, smacking the air where a large bug hovered, wings loudly buzzing.

The big cat missed it entirely.

Great hunter my pale behind.

I realized the bug was Sebille as she flew over the yellow tape, heading directly for the spot where the body appeared to have been.

The sprite was about the size of a dragonfly, her wings a beautiful mix of iridescent purple and green that created a rainbow blur on the air as she buzzed back and forth over the spot on the ground. Then she stopped and hovered over the spot, a soft pink glow extending downward from her wingtips in an irregular shape that reached to the ground and hung there, throbbing softly in time with her wings.

The Enchanted cop on the other side of the park

suddenly flinched, straightening away from the playground structure where he'd been leaning, and starting forward. "Hey! What are you doing there?"

The sprite shot straight into the air, the magic glow dissipating in a swirling wisp of energy that blew away on a soft breeze. She disappeared into the dense branches of a large tree, her light extinguished.

I pictured her sitting on a branch like a tiny bird, obscured by the dense tangle of branches and leaves, and smiled. I'd give anything to have wings like that. To be able to just fly away when trouble threatened.

"Come on." Alice grabbed my arm and jerked me sideways, ripping me from my daydreams.

I stumbled after her as the cop yelled something in our direction, my gaze sliding back to him. He was on his cell, and his expression was mutinous. He'd clearly connected the disruption of his crime scene with us, though I had no idea how.

"What's going on?" I asked Alice.

She shook her head, risking a quick look at the cop. "Just hurry, will you?"

Behind us, Fenwald loped heavily along the sidewalk, occasionally going vertical to smack at a passing bug and yowl his displeasure when he missed. Every third time he jumped, he smacked into my calves, his weight throwing me off enough to make me stumble. I turned to glare at him. "Stop that, you silly cat."

He narrowed his silvery-green gaze on me and yowled unrepentantly, his tattered tail snapping the air with insolence.

When we'd gone two full blocks down the street, Alice finally slowed and turned to look back the way we'd come. Some of the tension left her face and she relaxed. "We can wait here."

"For what?" I asked, and then swiped at a large bug that buzzed past my ear. The bug hovered on the air a few feet away, hands on hips and tiny face filled with irritation.

"Oh," I said.

Sebille popped back to full size and rolled her eyes. "Watch where you're swinging that hand."

"Sorry."

"What did you discover?" Alice asked.

"The magic signature has been expunged."

I had no idea what that meant, but whatever it was had Alice's eyes going round. "Magically?"

Sebille shrugged. "It appears so, yes."

Alice wrapped her arms around herself and stared at the cracked concrete under her feet. She seemed really upset by the news.

"What does that mean?" I asked.

Sebille's lids twitched as if she were fighting off an eye-roll at my ignorance. But she must have decided to take pity on me and offer information instead of disdain. "It means a supernormal messed with it to hide the identity of the killer."

"What kind of supernormal could do that?" I asked.

"A witch. A wizard." Alice slid her gaze thoughtfully toward me. "A sorcerer."

"Does Gnomish have a mage on staff?" Sebille asked.

Alice's gaze shot in her direction. "You think Gnomish killed him?"

"I think we need to consider it. Whoever killed that gnome, it was professionally done." She slid her glance along the street. "I doubt he was murdered by a baker, a shoe salesman..." She swung the hand toward a slim, dark-haired man leaving one of the storefronts. "Or a travel agent."

I didn't know about those businesses, but I was pretty sure I knew a pair of flip flops that could have gotten the job done. I shook off that thought and the feelings of inadequacy it engendered. "Maybe Gnomish was mad at him for causing a scene in front of Croakies," I said. "It sounds like they wanted to keep a low profile. Duking it out with Alice on the street wasn't exactly conducive to impressing potential customers."

"Especially since I kicked his butt," Alice agreed with a saucy grin.

Sebille shrugged her shoulders. "There's one more thing."

Alice and I fixed her with matching expectant stares.

"The grass was long in that park, and it rained last night, so the weight of the body made a pretty good impression."

We waited for her to explain what that had to do with anything. She frowned, seeming uncomfortable with what she was about to tell us.

"Yes, and...?" Alice nudged.

"And that impression was nearly a perfect rectangle. No human-like rounded parts or bumps. There were some indentations in the middle, but the edges were almost completely straight."

"What does that mean?" I asked.

Sebille shrugged. "Your guess is as good as mine. But I'm going to take a wild guess here and say..." She took a deep breath. "Your dead guy was smashed into something rectangular, about thirty-three by twenty-something inches. And he stayed inside whatever it was long enough for his body to take its shape."

I looked at Alice and she looked back, speculation running deep behind her oversized glasses.

I was pretty sure I knew exactly what rectangular thing poor Gido had been pressed into.

And, from Alice's sudden chalky pallor, I was pretty sure she did too.

11

BAD DAY?

A lice finally bought me those tacos she'd promised. Mostly because when she offered to pay the sprite back for her help, the cheeky red-haired woman all but demanded to be repaid in tacos.

She and I formed a permanent bond at that moment.

Alice seemed more annoyed by the request than pleased about getting off lightly. Which made me think she'd never intended to get me those tacos in the first place.

She'd probably thought she could buy me off with a bowl of gruel, a.k.a. pale, tasteless beans, or another dental disaster from the pastry-ish family.

Sebille and I were happily snarfing down our fourth taco each when the front door of Croakies opened and Grym the Grump walked inside, his handsome face set into a seemingly permanent scowl.

The detective's dark brows arched in surprise when he spotted the sprite. But he quickly recovered, turning to Alice. "I understand you tried to debauch my crime scene today."

Alice snorted out a laugh, spitting taco contents at Sebille and me. I took a tomato chunk to the nose, but the sprite had faster reflexes. Flinging up a protective napkin, Sebille handily blocked the cheese and lettuce mixture with her name on it. "We did no such thing, Detective," Alice argued with a secret smile. "Unless standing on a sidewalk looking at a rectangle of smashed grass is now considered debauching."

He sighed, rubbing a hand over his weary face. "You and I both know your intent."

Alice's smile widened. "You can't arrest me for intent."

He nodded, surprising me. I'd thought the old boy had more fight in him than that. "Bad day?" I asked before I realized the words were going to escape my mouth.

He sighed. "A long one." He cast his gaze on the greasy bag of tacos in the center of the table. "You don't have any of those to spare, do you?"

Alice nodded and stood, picking up her trash. "Have a seat. Do you want some tea?"

Sebille surged to her feet. "I'd be happy to make

it." The sprite sent me a pleading look. She must have heard how bad Alice's tea and...well everything else she fixed...was.

"That would be great," I said, avoiding Alice's gaze. "I'd love some too, Sebille."

"Brilliant," Alice said, dropping into Sebille's abandoned chair. "Any progress on the case?"

Grym pulled the bag closer and retrieved a taco, carefully unwrapping it and adding two packets of sauce before answering. "Other than the odd condition of the corpse..." He eyed us. "Which, I'm guessing you already figured out since you sent the sprite over the scene to view it..."

Yep, there was no moss growing on Detective Grym and Grouchy.

"We know it was pressed into a rectangle that was about three feet by two feet," Alice agreed, sending me a warning glance.

It wasn't necessary to warn me off elaborating. No good would come from EPD knowing the suitcase that had probably contained the corpse had been in the artifact library for the better part of a day before being liberated by magical means. "Have you ever seen anything like that before," I asked him.

He took his time chewing and swallowing. And then promptly took another bite, staring at me as he chewed.

The message in his eyes was clear as a bell. He wasn't going to tell.

But that was okay because his unwillingness to answer my question was all the answer I needed. "Any idea who killed him?"

Grym swallowed again, reaching for the bag.

I slammed my hand down on it and his gaze met mine, locking on.

I raised my brows.

Apparently, he was really hungry because he opened those perfect lips and said, "We're looking into the possibility that Gnomish had him taken out."

I was so surprised by his announcement I forgot to hold onto the bag, and he wrenched it away from me. I'd get nothing more from him until his next taco was gone.

"We were thinking along the same lines," Alice admitted.

Grym's gaze slid from mine. "Why?"

She shrugged. "Probably the same reasons you were."

He swallowed. "Humor me."

Sebille set a cup of tea in front of the detective. "Gnomish runs a protection racket," the sprite told him. "It's a company of thugs."

"Go on," he told her.

She gave me a steaming cup that smelled wonderful. I inhaled deeply over the chipped china, my eyes closing in pleasure. The tea smelled like heaven. Or magic.

"The scene with Alice in front of this place wasn't good for their business. Gnomish would know this," Sebille responded. "By killing Gido and dumping his body on the street, they send a message while removing any perceived weakness in their organization."

Grym swallowed and glanced at the taco bag before looking at me.

"Go ahead," I told him. I was too busy enjoying my tea to deprive him of sustenance. "This tea is so good," I told the sprite. "What did you do to it?"

Sebille shrugged. "Nothing."

Grym groaned in pleasure. "She's right, you must have added something. Maybe just a titch of magic?"

She shook her head. "Nothing. I'm tea talented."

"You definitely are," Grym the Formerly Grumpy agreed.

Alice sipped her tea and gave Sebille a thumbs up. "Have you talked to Gnomish yet?"

Grym prepped his taco. "No. It's too delicate."

"Delicate?" Sebille asked, her skinny form going rigid with anger. "What does that mean?"

"It means the owner of the company is friends with the Mayor. It means the company is hands-off unless we can find indisputable evidence that they're involved."

"But how are you going to do that if you can't investigate them?" I asked.

"We can investigate, but we can't approach them

directly. And we have to be careful not to set off any alarm bells with our approach."

"Banshee boogers!" I said. "That's crazy."

He nodded. "Welcome to the world of politics and cronyism."

"I say we go in," Sebille said. She scraped a piece of lettuce off one tooth and sipped her tea, looking very relaxed in the chair. Like she wasn't planning on leaving any time soon.

I yawned. "In where?"

"Gnomish," she told me, about half disgusted with me for having to ask.

"That's a brilliant idea!" Alice agreed, her eyes lighting with interest behind her glasses.

Oliver was sitting on her shoulder again, blinking blank eyes at us and working his tiny throat. Fenwald was in his favorite spot, draped along the wide sill beneath the front window, his tail hanging limply toward the ground.

I couldn't see anything in the glass except our reflection, but the big cat appeared to be watching something. "Do you mean sneak in?" I had no idea what we could possibly gain from such a scandalous act. I, for one, didn't know how to begin looking for proof that they'd killed Gido.

"Sure. Why not?" the sprite said. "I doubt they've

even got decent security there. They're used to being the big bad wolf in the neighborhood. It probably wouldn't occur to them that they might need security".

Alice rubbed her hands together. "Let's do it tonight."

I started shaking my head, but Sebille beat me to it. "Not tonight. We need to plan for this."

Alice's face fell. "What's to plan? We just need to get inside the building and find something that documents the hit on Gido. How hard could it be?"

If I hadn't been so tired, I would have laughed. "You think they just wrote it down on a piece of paper? Bad guy checklist: Scare innocents, check. Befriend the Mayor so we don't get caught, check. Stuff Gido into a suitcase and dump his rectangular corpse in the park, check."

Sebille rolled her eyes, but I wasn't sure if it was at Alice or me. "We'll need to do this magically."

Oliver scampered down Alice's arm to her hand, blinking at me as if he was considering pretending I was a tree.

I shook my head, raising my hands above the table. "Nuh, uh, mister. I'm not a frog person."

Alice looked shocked. "Why ever not? Frogs are adorable."

I grimaced. I'd had a bad experience with one once. "I'm more of a cat person," I told her, hoping she didn't get her feelings hurt, but not caring enough to let her frog crawl all over me.

Fenwald suddenly jumped to his feet and yowled, his tail slapping the air behind him.

Sebille surged out of her chair.

"What's wr..." I started to ask.

I never got the words out.

As Sebille lifted her hands and sent a pale green wall of magic toward the window, something smacked into it from the outside. Something big that sounded like a freight train crashing into the building.

Fenwald flew away from the window on a yowl, his long legs pushing the air as he was propelled like a furry rocket into the room. Beside me, Alice made an "umph!" sound and fell backward off her chair with the furry projectile tucked against her middle.

I jumped to my feet.

The window bowed inward in a curved bubble that boiled with black energy, the glass making terrifying crackling noises as the oily power shoving it inward roared and pushed.

Sebille's face was a study in determination as the energy pressed closer. The window bowed inward until it had to be reaching its breaking point, groaning as the magic tried to expand it past the point the sprite's magic could contain it.

But her magic, which smelled of flowers and freshly-broken blades of grass, somehow managed to hold the energy back, bolstering the strained glass as it continued to bulge inward until I thought there was no way it could keep from breaking.

It didn't occur to me to hide. I stood there, transfixed by the horror show in front of me. If Sebille's energy failed and the window exploded inward, I'd be dead. But so would Sebille, and it seemed unfair to run to safety when she was risking herself trying to save us.

Unfortunately, there was nothing I could do except offer moral support. So I stood there, my hands lifting toward the bulging glass in silent support of her efforts.

My palms stung and a slim ribbon of pale gray energy slid from each of them, hitting the wall of green energy and mingling with it. It was too little to do much good. But it gave me an idea. I looked down at Alice. "Help her! Use your Keeper energy."

The glass crackled ominously. The sulfurous stench of ugly energy filled the room. The horrible smell made my eyes water and my stomach roll with nausea.

Alice gently pushed Fenwald off her stomach and tucked Oliver into her hair, shoving to her feet. Without another word, she stood between Sebille and me and raised her palms, sending dual ribbons of silvery magic into the pale green barrier keeping the window from shattering into a million tiny pieces.

The glass groaned, bulging another fraction of an inch inward, and then slowly started to ease backward under our combined efforts.

The roaring beyond the window started to soften, easing away into the night as the window steadily returned to normal.

And then the three of us collapsed onto the well-worn carpet and lay there, panting in exhaustion.

Alice didn't stay down long. She pushed to her feet and went over to the door, performing a complex spell that sealed Croakies from the magical influence of anyone except a Keeper. Then she slid, gray-faced, to the floor, resting her head against the door's smooth surface.

"What in the name of the goddess's favorite soup crackers was that?" I panted out.

Sebille's gaze caught mine, the iridescent green swirling with residual energy. "I don't know for sure, but I'll bet I can guess."

Alice nodded, reaching inside the pocket of her sweater for her phone. "I can guess too. But Lea should be able to tell us for sure."

12

FI FIDDLE FOE, TO GNOMISH WE WILL GO

L ea gathered up her candles and broke the edge of the circle with her toe. "There's no doubt in my mind this is the same mage," she told us.

The verification was terrifying. Apparently, whoever had invaded Croakies to steal the suitcase wasn't done with us. "Why do you suppose he attacked?" I asked the three other women.

Sebille shrugged.

Lea didn't respond, apparently thinking my question had been for the others.

Alice chewed on her bottom lip, her gaze skittering guiltily away.

"What aren't you telling us?" I asked, frowning. She could keep her little secrets if they only affected her. But if Lea, Sebille, and I were going to get sucked into a black magic vortex because of something she'd done, Alice owed it to us to come clean.

The Keeper's jaw turned mulish, and her small eyes flashed with anger. "Why would you think I'm not telling you something?" she asked angrily.

"Maybe because you're looking guiltier than a puppy piddling on a newly mopped floor?" Sebille offered wryly.

Alice jammed her hands onto her hips and stared us all down for a beat, and then seemed to realize it wasn't working and sighed. "I didn't get an order on the suitcase."

Sebille and Lea frowned in confusion.

I thought about her admission for a beat and then realized the significance. "It wasn't supposed to be here?"

Alice shook her head. "It showed up in the bookstore a few days ago, and I should have looked into why. But I was...busy."

I was starting to realize that Alice was always busy. Unfortunately, it seemed she was rarely busy doing actual Keeper work. "So you just added it to the pile of artifacts to be cataloged," I said, giving her a hostile stare.

"I could feel its magic," she admitted. "But it didn't seem malevolent. I assumed the Universe had just forgotten to give me an order on it...or that it was a revoked artifact."

"Revoked artifact?" Lea asked.

Woo, was I happy she'd asked instead of me.

"When an artifact is lost or is being misused, I

generally get an order for its retrieval. But sometimes the situation is too dire, or wires get crossed in
the system and the Universe just does a special
retrieval, dumping it in my lap," Alice explained.

My eyes went wide. "Crossed wires? Does that
happen very often?"

Alice chewed her bottom lip. "No. I personally
have only had it happen one time. But other Keepers
I've spoken to have experienced it, so it's not all that
rare."

I knew from Alice's whirlwind instruction on the
first day that each dimensional space had its own
Keeper of the Artifacts, or KoA. But each dimension
only had one. Along with a Universal governing
body that ruled from an undetermined central place
where they kept watch on all of the dimensional
representatives, Keepers answered to a ruling body
of Powers that Be, which, in turn, answered to the
Universe. Like Keepers, there was only one PTB per
dimensional space, and outside of extraordinary
circumstances, they weren't allowed to cross into
another PTB's dimension or interfere with their
activities.

I wasn't exactly sure how the Société of Dire
Magic fit into the hierarchy, except that they seemed
to be more of an educational organization than a
disciplinary one. Though Alice had told me they'd
stepped into a policing role on occasion, when it was
deemed necessary.

"But that still doesn't explain why the mage is attacking you," Sebille said, her brows like accusatory slashes above a galaxy of freckles.

Alice paled. "I might have put a Keeper's Mark on the suitcase before I stashed it."

Lea gasped. "You didn't!"

Alice twitched her lips to the side.

"What's that?" I asked, a sense of foreboding filling me.

When Alice didn't immediately respond, Lea said, "It's an invisible mark that, once added to an artifact, makes it all but unusable."

I thought about that. "So the mage probably took it back to his lair and tried to use it, then realized what you'd done..."

"And returned to make her remove it," Sebille finished for me. She frowned. "But my understanding was that it could never be safely removed once placed on a magical object."

Alice turned an odd shade of green.

"So why attack us?" I asked, wondering what the big deal was. "Why does it matter that the suitcase is nil? What could the thing have done that would be important enough to potentially kill three people?"

"Because artifacts, especially the dangerous ones, are generally geared toward gaining love, wealth, or power. Things people kill for all the time. And because there's only one way to remove a Keeper's Mark once it's placed," Alice said.

By the twitchy aspect of her movements and the greenish hue of her homely face, I was pretty sure I knew what that one way was. "You have to die," I said, my voice catching on the words.

Alice sighed.

Lea shook her head. "Killing Alice *might* disrupt the mark, but it's not guaranteed. And if it doesn't work, the last option is negated."

"What's that?" I asked.

"The Keeper can always open the artifact," Sebille said, her gaze locked on my face. She seemed to be waiting for me to understand.

It took me a minute but I finally did. "Ah. Oh! He'll try to take Alice and force her to open it."

"Yes," Sebille agreed. "And he won't be content with a one time open. He'll try to keep her prisoner."

Alice's green color deepened.

"What happens to the mark if you pass the Keeper position to Naida?" Lea asked Alice.

"I'm not sure. As far as I know, it's never been tested."

All the blood ran out of my face until I no doubt matched Alice. "You mean this guy's going to try to kill or kidnap me too?"

Nobody looked at me. Trying to catch their gazes was like trying to capture a lightning bug with a floppy hat.

I narrowed my gaze on Sebille. "What do you know about this?" I asked the sprite.

"Not much. My people haven't had any experience with a Keeper's Mark that I'm aware of. But I can ask my mother." She looked at Alice and the Keeper nodded.

"Thanks," she said, looking sincerely grateful. "Maybe she'll know of a way to break it." Alice didn't need to add the unspoken thought, "without anyone having to die."

"We can try Madeline Quilleran," Lea said, dread clear in her voice.

Alice flinched as if struck. "I'd rather not if we can avoid it."

"Who's that?" I asked.

"One of the most powerful witches in the country," Lea said, frowning. "She's a little scary."

"Why is she scary?"

"In general, the Quillerans are not what anybody would consider light witches. They dabble in blood magic and tend toward the black side of the magic arts," Lea explained.

"Madeline's not a black witch," Alice said, sounding defensive.

Lea just shook her head.

"Have you worked with her?" I asked Alice.

"Yes. She actually created an impenetrable security system for Croakies. It's completely Keeper initiated and controlled."

Lea nodded. "She's got a reputation for helping

the magic community on occasion. But it always has to be on her terms."

"Back to the current problem," Sebille said. "How are we going to find this mage so we can stop him?"

Alice rubbed her arms. "I...um...might have an idea where the suitcase is. I'm assuming if we find that, we'll find him."

"Good," I said. I'd ask her later how she knew where it was. I was assuming it had something to do with the mark she'd put on it. "Where is it?"

"It's um..." She twitched for a moment, her gaze sliding around the room, and then hugged herself as if she were cold. "It's at Gnomish."

"Well," I said, sucking down the fact that I wasn't going to be getting sleep any time soon. "I guess we're going to Gnomish then."

———

Other than the two-story-high red, yellow, and white garden gnome gracing the grassy center of the circular drive in front of the gray brick building, Gnomish, Inc. looked just like any other professional business.

The parking lot to the side of the building was empty.

"Nobody here. Maybe they don't have a security guard," I said, frowning.

"Maybe," Sebille agreed. "If there is, I'll deal with him."

Her "take no prisoners" attitude had me a little concerned. "What exactly does that mean?" I asked. I was all for helping Alice with her problem...especially since it was probably going to become *my* problem if it wasn't solved...but I had no intention of going to prison for committing gnomicide, thank you very much.

Sebille's silent shrug did *not* make me feel better.

No, it did not.

Alice parked her frumpy white sedan in the shadows near the building and we climbed out. "How are we getting inside?" I asked.

Alice looked at Sebille. The sprite expelled an irritated sigh and rolled her eyes. No small feat when performed simultaneously. A beat later, she'd popped into dragonfly size and buzzed toward the building. We listened to her buzzing along the face of the building for several minutes before a tinny whisper sifted down to us. "I've found an open window. I'll get the lay of the land and let you in."

Alice took a deep breath as if she'd been holding it.

The two of us stood there for a minute, the silence stretched taut between us.

As usual, I was the one to break it. "We'll figure this out," I told the Keeper.

Alice glanced my way, her expression unreadable

in the dim light. But she bobbed her head in agreement and surprised me by giving my hand a squeeze. "Thanks for helping me with this."

I smiled to show her it was okay, then realized she probably couldn't see it. "It's fine. I'm glad I can help in some way." Though I had no idea *how* I could help. I was really just along for moral support. Or, remembering the giant hot fudge brownie sundae I'd scarfed before coming to Gnomish, for ballast.

"I'm sorry I didn't tell you about the suitcase."

So was I. But if I was honest with myself, I wouldn't have been able to do anything about it anyway.

We stood in silence for a few moments, an icy wind scouring the flat ground of the business park just outside of Enchanted. Almost simultaneously, Alice and I pulled our coats closer and turned away from it. The brittle air had the smell of snow in it and I found myself anticipating the change. I'd always loved snow. Even though I'd never been a fan of cold weather.

The lock turned on the front door and it swung open.

Sebille's bony frame was backlit by the soft lighting of the lobby. "Come on!" she urged impatiently.

We hurried into the building and she locked it behind us. "I haven't seen a guard," she whispered.

Then she looked at Alice. "Where do you want to start?"

Alice glanced around, outwardly calm.

I was only half paying attention because the place was already creeping me out. The walls were lined with statues of garden gnomes, their dark eyes blank and dead. Their smiles looked evil in the low light. "Creepy," I told my companions.

Sebille barely spared them a glance. "We should hurry."

Alice nodded, pointing to the center of the lobby, which was open to the second and third levels.

I took a step in that direction and there was a soft whoosh of air, followed by a quick flash of scarlet light.

We stilled, waiting.

Nothing else happened.

I looked at Alice.

"It was probably an alarm spell," she told me as if it was nothing. "Someone will come soon. We need to hurry."

I felt every drop of blood fleeing from my face, sprinting down my veins into my heart and lungs, where it started a riot that made everything in my chest clench and roar.

Every instinct I owned was screaming at me to get out of that building.

Telling me to run.

Run fast.

But Sebille and Alice started forward and, not knowing what else to do, I followed them.

The open area on the main floor contained a raised octagonal greenspace with an enormous tree in its center. The tree's lush-leafed branches reached high and wide into the open space.

Around the tree was an assortment of flowering plants, the leaves shiny and dense, and the blooms vivid against their vibrant green hues. My gaze scanning the darkness high above our heads, I got a sense of banister-lined walkways in the dim lighting. My imagination conjured a series of doors forming the backside of the hovering walkways. The Gnomish, Inc. offices.

"I'll send out my Keeper energy from here," Alice explained to me. "So it can travel through the whole building."

I bit back an urge to tell her to get to it. The back of my neck was prickling uneasily. I couldn't help feeling like somebody was watching us.

Probably those stupid, mean-eyed statues.

Alice lifted her hands and dipped her head back, her eyes glowing with silver light. Matching silver energy shimmered into existence above her outstretched palms and sifted into the dark above our heads.

Her glowing eyes had me taking a step back. Did I look like that when I sent out my fledgling magics? Nah, I decided. I didn't have enough magic inside me to even make my eyes sparkle, let alone glow.

Sebille and I watched as dual ribbons of silvery energy wound upward from her hands, into the open space above our heads.

We stood in silence for a moment, waiting. A beat later, a distant chime sounded. It appeared to have come from the top floor. Alice hurried toward the staircase that led to the dim levels above, and we started up.

By the time we stepped off the stairs into the hallway on level three, I was panting like a puppy in August and my heart was pounding. It felt like I was going to have a heart attack.

That was the moment I realized I would need to get into better shape to do my job. Maybe eat fewer tacos. It was ridiculous to be so out of shape at twenty-two.

"Any idea which office?" Sebille asked Alice.

Alice lifted her hands, palms pointed toward the ceiling, and her eyes glowed silver again. A beat later, she seemed to shake herself out of her daze. "The door at the end of the hall."

We hurried toward the door she'd indicated, finding it locked. With a sigh, Sebille popped small again and shoved her way through a mail slot in the door. A beat later the lock turned, and she let us into what looked like the offices of an executive.

The small front room had appealing hardwood

flooring in a weathered gray. A round, burgundy rug dominated the center of the space, and black leather bucket chairs were arranged along the walls.

The portrait hanging on the wall above a shiny gray receptionist's desk was of a distinguished-looking gnome, whose long, pointed beard and bushy eyebrows were pure white. The nose above a pair of flowing mustaches was round and red, and the cheeks were a healthy pink color.

The small blue eyes sparkled, making the gnome look harmless and friendly. But the cruel slash of lips told me that was a ruse. I moved close to the painting and examined the brass plate centered on the bottom section of the heavy wood frame. It read, Gerrard Gnomish Senior.

I glanced at Sebille, who'd come up beside me. "This is the owner of the company?"

She shrugged. "Who knows. Those guys all look the same to me."

She wasn't wrong. Though I had a feeling the man in the painting wouldn't appreciate the sentiment. He looked very proud of himself.

"It's down here," Alice said, pointing down a short hallway. We passed a door with a bubbled glass window, noting the darkness behind the glass. I read the nameplate on the door and realized it belonged to Mr. Gnomish himself. Or maybe it was Junior Gnomish. If there was a Junior.

Squelching the desire to open the door and peek

inside, I hurried after Alice. Sebille stayed behind, her gaze sliding suspiciously toward the door. "Hurry up," she told us. "I have a bad feeling about this place."

Alice stopped in front of a second door, one without any glass, and grabbed the handle. She yanked it open without hesitation. For a single heartbeat, nothing happened. Silence throbbed down the hall and Alice stood staring into the space she'd exposed, her eyes alight with silvery energy.

Then everything happened at once.

The lights in the office snapped on, filling every nook with eye-stinging light.

As if she hadn't noticed the light, Alice reached through the door.

That red light we'd seen downstairs flared again, brief and uneventful.

"Found it," Alice chirped happily.

Then the lights snapped off, leaving us light-blind as the walls around us seemed to boil with energy.

I started backing away from the door where Alice stood, holding the familiar suitcase. "We need to go," I told her, fear throbbing in my voice.

She turned to look at me, her face an amorphous blur to my light-blind eyes. I was pretty sure she nodded.

And then something shot out of the place where she'd found the suitcase. There was a roar and Alice sailed backward, smacking hard against the wall across from the door. A soft click sounded above my head and I glanced up. Mistake. *Big* mistake. A thunderous stream of water roared down on me, hitting me with the force of a baseball bat and sending me to the floor. The water pounded against my skin, bashing my head against the hard floor every time I tried to lift it. I struggled to breathe beneath its onslaught.

Oddly, there was no puddle beneath me. Instead, a sweet, flowery scent rose up to fill my senses.

I heard Sebille cry out behind me, but the water held me on the ground, relentless and painful against my skin.

Finally, the gusher shut off and I forced myself to move, though my body was battered and sore, as if I'd been pounded from head-to-toe by an angry gorilla. I pushed to my knees and looked down in surprise at the thick covering of flower petals across the floor.

Flowers? What in the name of the goddess's favorite spatula was going on?

Alice groaned, the sound prolonged and filled with pain.

My gaze jerked to the spot where she huddled against the floor. The suitcase lay on its side nearby, covered in flowers.

I shoved to my feet and ran to her.

There were sounds of fighting behind us, and I knew Sebille was in trouble.

"Come on, Alice. Sebille needs help."

She let me pull her to her feet, shoving a thick mop of hair off her face and scrubbing a hand over her dripping face. I watched in amazement as the droplets of water she shed turned to petals as they hit the floor.

She must have seen the wonder on my face and shook her head. "Garden magic. The water only attacks flesh and blood creatures. When it comes into contact with non-biologics, it turns to flora."

A slash of green energy sliced down the hallway, exploding in a flash of light a few feet away. Alice grabbed the suitcase and we ran toward the receptionist's lobby.

I had no idea what I was going to be seeing once we got there. The dark ahead was fractured by bursts of green and orange light. The stench of sulfur filled the air, along with the strong scent of flowers and herbs.

As we ran into the lobby, Sebille screamed, "Watch out!"

We dove to the ground as energy slashed through the air where we'd been. I scurried behind one of the chairs lining the wall, and Alice scrambled the opposite direction, diving underneath the desk as another bolt of magic tried to dissect her.

I watched in amazement as Sebille exchanged

bolts of energy with something in the corner. Peering around the chair, I looked around for her nemesis, finding only a haze of smog and a potted plant with oversized, dark green leaves.

Whoever it was must be hiding behind the plant, I decided.

Then the leaves twisted and a large yellow flower emerged from their midst. Sebille, in her dragonfly-sized sprite form, buzzed behind the desk as a jolt of black energy shot from the flower and seared across the wall behind where she'd been.

She was fighting the flower? I blinked in surprise and, I'll admit it, a little fascination. The world I'd entered was truly amazing.

And deadly.

I couldn't forget that part.

I looked at Sebille, who was keeping the desk between her and the angry blossom. "What do you want us to do?"

The flower sent several bolts of its deadly energy into the desk, propelling pieces of it into the air in jagged strips.

In a moment of pure clarity, I realized it was trying to get to Alice.

Sebille dodged low to the ground and buzzed over to me, landing on my shoulder. She smelled of flowers and green growing things. "What's going on?" I asked.

"What's going on is that we're not getting out of here with that suitcase," she responded angrily.

I frowned. I couldn't imagine why Gnomish, Inc. would be so determined to hold onto an old suitcase artifact that it would use deadly force to keep it.

I suddenly wished I knew exactly what that suitcase could do.

Alice's face appeared at the end of the desk. The plant fired several more times, shearing off another chunk of her barrier. "It's all gone to pot, ladies," she said. "We need to scamper."

Sebille rolled her eyes. "Now, why didn't I think of that."

13

WELL, THIS IS A BIT OF A DAMP SQUIB I'NT?

Sebille and I ducked as another round of energy blasted into the chair we were hiding behind. It blew the chair backward, turning me into a greasy splat on the wall.

Sebille cannonballed skyward before the plant had a chance to refocus and plunged downward, hitting the dirt in the planter and sending it into the air in a tiny brown geyser.

Almost immediately, the dirt lit up in a green haze that sent the plant into paroxysms of vibrating and wobbling. The frantic flailing had the plant's wooden "arms" banging against the wall in an unsuccessful effort to rid itself of the "bug" infestation.

Energy seeped downward from the surface of the soil, even as dirt continued to geyser upward, painting the floor around the plant in a dusting of dirt.

With a final, violent wobble that nearly toppled it to the ground, the plant finally went still, its stalk doubling over and shriveling up as if it had been dead for weeks.

Gasping and coughing up dust, the sprite burst from the soil and flew my way with dirt sifting off her wings.

In a blast of light and flower-scented energy, Sebille popped back into her human size. Wiping mud from her eyes, she headed for the door. "Come on, the alert has gone out. There will be a lot more trouble between us and the door."

Alice emerged from behind the desk, the suitcase bouncing against her leg as she ran toward the door. I scraped myself off the wall and followed, wondering what in the world I'd gotten myself into.

It didn't take long for me to find out.

Sebille cracked the door open and glanced around. Then she turned back to us and nodded, holding her finger to her lips for quiet.

She didn't have to tell me twice. After being nearly drowned by flower petals and obliterated by a potted plant, I'd slither down the hall on my belly if I thought it would get us safely out of that horrible place.

We followed Sebille down the hall toward the

stairs. She jolted to a stop on the top step, her body going rigid.

I peeked over her shoulder and gave a quiver of alarm.

The area at the bottom of the stairs was filled with waiting forms, their postures rigid and their gazes sparking with hostility.

The sinister cast to their lips had changed, becoming more menacing as they waited in silence. There were dozens of them, and every wooden face was focused on us.

It was the gnomes that had lined the wall in the lobby. Each one holding a spade, or a shovel, or a deadly-looking three-pronged cultivator in their knobby wooden grips.

Alice peered over Sebille's other shoulder and grimaced. "Well, this is a bit of a damp squib I'nt?" she murmured softly.

Sebille snorted out a laugh. "A bit. Any suggestions?"

We shared a look. I was at a loss. Alice shrugged. Sebille sighed. "Alice, is that suitcase worth dying over?" she finally asked.

To my shock, Alice seemed to be giving that some thought. Finally, she said simply, "Yes."

Sebille sighed again. "Okay, this is what we've got. Those things are wooden soldiers."

My mind went blank on her words, picturing

harmless toys that were safe for toddlers to play with.

She looked into my blank expression and rolled her eyes.

I was really getting tired of the rolling eyes thing. It was giving me a complex. I clamped down on the desire to remind her I was only two days into the job. But I was all too painfully aware of my inadequate knowledge of magic and magic users. I realized I should have been more curious growing up. As soon as I noticed the anomalies...the odd items following me around...the way electronic devices went snowy and jumped around when I passed by...I should have looked into the magic background I knew was my hereditary legacy.

I'd been a coward. And now I needed the Wizard to give me courage. "What does that mean?" I asked.

"They're similar to a golem, but they're made of wood." Alice narrowed her gaze on me. "You do know what a golem is, right?"

Only about half, but I nodded. "Are they dangerous?"

"Very," Sebille said. "They have only one purpose, and they don't stop until they achieve it. They're nearly impermeable. They're formed of wood from a magical forest. They can't be cut, burned, drowned or shot."

"And don't forget they have very sharp garden implements in their hands," Alice said, grimacing.

"So, what you're telling me is that we're as corked as the goddess's favorite wine?" I asked.

"Basically," Alice agreed, almost cheerfully.

"We have to have options," I whined unprofessionally. My mind raced over the possibilities as silence descended once again.

Sebille finally said. "They're not sentient in the way we think of it. They don't rationalize or adjust. They just lock on and go."

A thought occurred to me. "What if we didn't look like their intended victims?"

Both Alice and Sebille frowned in confusion.

I didn't know much, but I did know some things. For example, I knew that sprites were good for gardens. Which meant she probably had some skill in growing things. I eyed the enormous tree, whose branches reached toward the stairway with knobby fingers.

Knobby, *strong* fingers.

"What if we were covered in leaves or...flowers?" I asked, warming to my idea. "Would they still recognize us?"

Sebille thought about this for a beat and then nodded. "It might work." She followed my line of sight to the tree, her gaze going speculative.

Unfortunately, our time for discussing and considering was over.

With a long, wailing roar that made my skin crawl and ice coat my brain, the wooden army below us broke its waiting stance and barreled up the stairway toward us.

"The tree!" Sebille yelled unnecessarily.

I was shocked and appalled by how quickly the blocky little soldiers conquered the stairs. In the blink of an eye, they'd cut the distance between us nearly in half, and the stairway shook beneath their combined movement and weight.

Sebille leaped easily across the four-foot space between the stairs and the tree. Hands clasping a sturdy branch, she swung her body lithely to sit astride it, her gaze locked on the quickly ascending army of short, widely-made wooden soldiers. "Hurry up!" she yelled at Alice and me.

We climbed over the railing, teetering on the few inches of exposed stair beyond the railing. The first gnome hit the landing only five steps below us, and Alice leaped, her panicked scream turning shrill enough to hurt my ears.

My head whiplashing back and forth between the approaching gnomes and Alice, I watched in horror as the Keeper fell past the branch she'd been aiming for, her fingertips barely grazing it and then slipping away as she dropped like a rock toward the ground.

I screamed her name, my own voice matching hers for screechiness.

The branch below the one she missed suddenly

swerved sideways, breaking her fall and wrapping its smaller branches around her waist as she threatened to bounce off again.

I looked at Sebille and realized that had been her handiwork.

Shimmering green energy swirled around her outstretched hands, and the scent of Spring flowers wafted over me.

Her horrified green gaze sliced past me and widened.

That and the soft scuff of several pairs of shoes on the stair were the only warning I got that I was out of time.

"Jump!" Sebille screamed.

I didn't turn to see how close they were. Before I could think about the danger of leaping four feet to a branch that might or might not hold my weight, I jumped.

But I didn't go anywhere.

Several small, hard hands caught my arms before I was away, yanking me roughly backward. I slammed into a wall of painted wood and it gave way, tumbling back down the stairs with me riding them like a boat bouncing inelegantly over river rapids.

We clanged en masse into the railing at the landing that was several steps down, and the wooden "rapids" rolled out from underneath me as I fought to regain my feet.

Something hit me on the back of my neck, just below my skull, and pain scissored through me, creeping outward in a dull throb that made my knees and arms go limp for just a beat.

Another blow landed on my forehead. And another on my right shoulder. Several more hit me in quick succession, until all I could think to do was curl up into a ball and try to keep my most vulnerable parts protected.

The gnomes were eerily silent. The only noise for a long moment was the meaty sound of their little fists smacking against my flesh.

My cries were muffled by the fact that I was curled into a ball, my face buried in my chest and my arms forming a protective barrier around my head.

Metal clanged loudly above me, causing me to jerk and lift my head.

There was a shovel caught in the uprights of the railing. It was twisting and banging against the metal supports in an effort to get loose.

That was the moment when I knew staying in the fetal position wouldn't work. They were going to start attacking me with sharp metal implements any second.

I had to move.

Somehow.

The pile of wooden bodies had deepened on top of me. Their weight was more than I could simply shove away. The upside of that pileup was that it was harder for the gnomes with weapons to get to me.

Despite that, I couldn't risk staying there.

It was only a matter of time before one of those sharp blades found its way to me.

Alice screamed her shrill scream again, and the pile on top of me shifted, lightened, as some of the soldiers headed toward the sound.

I buried my worry for the Keeper behind my need to escape my current predicament. I wouldn't be any good to her if they hacked me into a million little pieces. I gathered myself, tightening my muscles in preparation for making my move, and then, as another scream sounded in the lobby below, I took a deep breath and shoved upward, sending gnomes flying away from me like cordwood. Some of them tumbled over the railing and thudded against the ground below.

But not enough.

They were on me again in the time it took for me to run across the landing. Hands grabbed at my calves, jerking me to a stop, and my arms flew up as my momentum threw my upper body forward even as my legs were yanked back.

"Naida!" Sebille screamed.

My head jerked up as something wrapped itself around my arms. My protective instincts, already in hyperdrive, slammed into high gear as I tried to jerk away. But the vines that entwined me were like steel.

There was no breaking through them without a blade.

I threw back my head and screamed, my voice throbbing with rage, as whatever had me in its grip wrapped its way down my body and to my hips. I struggled and kicked, trying to expel the gnomes, which were inexplicably still attacking me despite the fact that the vining had me firmly in its grip.

"Naida!" Sebille screamed again. "You have to stop fighting."

I was too frantic to listen. I struggled until I was coated in sweat, my body throbbing from the pain the gnomes had inflicted and the new damage I was doing to myself in the battle against the vines.

My feet left the ground, the vines carrying me toward the ceiling high above, and I was shocked into sudden silence.

"It's okay," Sebille yelled again. She was standing near the door, hands lifted and green energy bathing the air between her and the massive tree.

As I was lifted safely away from the gnomes, the vines a gentle, but firm vehicle for my flight toward the spot where Alice and Sebille waited, my gaze slid along the vining to where it began, wrapped around the trunk of the tree.

Sebille's magic.

Not the gnomes.

Thank the goddess. I expelled a breath that

carried some of my terror with it. And let myself go limp in the gentle grasp of the sprite's magic.

I was going to survive.

But holy hippopotamus in a Humvee, I was gonna be sore.

14

MAKE ME A MAGIC MUFFIN MISTER

I heard the bell clang through the library the next morning and knew I needed to get up, but my entire body felt like one giant bruise and I couldn't make myself do it.

Just the weight of the covers on my skin was causing agony to throb through me.

I lay there for a long moment, trying to open my eyes. It was like somebody had glued them shut. I finally gave up, started to roll over to get into a better position to go back to sleep, and sucked in a gasp as the pulsating pain suffusing my body exploded into tsunami-level misery.

I gave a little scream and went perfectly still.

A moment later, footsteps sounded on the concrete floor. I lay as still as I could, my eyes open and tears of pain sliding down my cheeks.

"Naida?" Alice's voice filtered toward me through the looming stacks of artifacts. "Are you okay?"

Moving only my eyes, I tracked her as she appeared from behind the shelves. When she saw me, her eyes went wide. "Blimey," she breathed.

I forced myself to speak, though I was afraid that moving my lips might set off another wave of torment. "I'm okay. Just a little sore."

She shook her head. "Rubbish. You look bloody awful. Stay there. I'll call Doctor Whom." She turned on her heel and clip-clopped away.

Thinking of the medicine the good doctor would be offering, I grimaced. We didn't really need any more rodents running around. "You don't need to," I called out, a tinge of desperation in my voice. But, per usual, Alice ignored me.

"Maybe he'll be too busy," I murmured sleepily, letting my eyes drift closed again. Sometime later, I jolted awake again to the sensation of heat running over my body. A sweet, floral scent filled the air and I recognized it as magic. My eyes jerked open in sudden panic. I jumped when I spotted the woman bending over me. "Sebille! You scared me."

She rolled her eyes. "You scared yourself." The sprite sat back, lines of weariness on her long, homely face as she stared at me. "How do you feel?"

I grimaced, hoping Sebille's presence there meant that Alice had been unable to contact the doc.

"I'm fine. Really. Will you help me talk Alice out of calling Doctor Whom?"

"Already done."

"He's busy and I..." My lips slammed closed as I realized I didn't need to convince her. "Oh. Thanks for that."

She frowned and continued to sit on the edge of the bed as if waiting for me to do something. I had no idea what. The one thing I really needed to do, I was pretty sure Sebille didn't want me to tell her about. "If you'll excuse me, I need to go to the ladies..." I shoved back the covers and sat up, jolting to a stop. My eyes went wide. "Wait... I'm not in agony all over my body anymore."

Sebille's lips curved slightly upward in the corners. She nodded once and stood. "I can go then."

I reached out and touched her hand. "You did this?"

She fidgeted nervously, looking uncomfortable at the idea of having to answer my question. Finally, she just shrugged.

"Thank you so much. This is amazing." I rolled my shoulders and then stretched my arms over my head. There was a slight tightness in my lower back, a touch of tenderness, but the pain was all but gone. "You're a goddess."

Sebille snorted out a laugh. "If you believe that, you haven't been paying attention. I'll see you up front when you're...erm..." She shrugged again. "See you in a few minutes."

I nodded, happy that she wasn't leaving Croakies. I wanted to pick her brain about everything that had happened the night before. And about the suitcase.

I wasn't sure how forthcoming Alice was going to be about it, and I wanted Sebille there to help me drag it out of her. The Keeper knew more than she was letting on about the artifact and what it did.

Which might mean she knew more about Gido's death than she was letting on too. The thought made me frown. "See you in a few."

A quick, hot shower and two cups of tea later, I narrowed my gaze on Alice. "What's up with the flushing situation up there?"

Alice laughed. "You don't like to sing?"

Sebille looked from one to the other of us, clearly confused.

I grimaced. "It's kind of tacky, don't you think?"

Alice laughed again, clearly enjoying herself. "It was like that when I got here. A previous Keeper having a bit of fun at our expense, I expect."

"What are you talking about?" Sebille asked.

I grinned. "The toilet in Alice's apartment doesn't

flush normally. You have to sing the *Make Me a Magic Muffin Mister* song while jiggling the handle for it to flush."

Sebille grimaced. "Ew."

I laughed at her reaction. "Yeah. It's pretty weird."

"I've never heard of that song," Sebille said. "How'd you know the words?"

"They're printed on the wall above the loo," Alice explained. "Enhanced with a spell, so the tune is inherent inside the lyrics."

Sebille settled back in her chair. "Okay, I'm intrigued. Sing it for me."

Alice and I shared a look and a smile. She gave me a little nod and we broke into song.

Make me a magic muffin mister. Make me a magic song. Don't forget to jiggle now, and you'll never get it wrong. Make me a magic muffin mister and don't be in a rush. Because if you don't sing the magic muffin song, you won't ever get a flush.

From above our heads came the sound of a toilet flushing. The toilet in the small bathroom at the back of the bookstore flushed shortly after that.

I laughed. "I didn't know the one down here was tied to the magic too. The flusher works normally."

Alice shrugged. "I added that when I came. It's handy."

Smiling widely, Sebille ate another bite of her donut. We ate and drank tea in companionable silence for a few minutes, until Sebille set her mug down on the table with a soft thump, her gaze sliding around the bookstore. "Where'd you put the suitcase?"

"Somewhere safe," Alice said evasively. "After the last time, I wasn't taking any chances."

I settled my gaze on Alice. "What's the deal with that thing, anyway? Why is everybody after it?"

Alice stared down at her tea. She was silent for long enough that I opened my mouth to nudge her. But she finally looked up, skimming a gaze from me to Sebille. "I should have been paying closer attention." She sighed. "It's one of a very few rare artifacts that have dimensional bending properties."

Sebille went very still, but I was confused. "What does that mean, exactly?"

"It means it's very dangerous. And very useful to the wrong element," Alice responded.

When I shook my head, lifting my hands in frustration, Sebille clarified what Alice seemed unwilling to share. "Plane bending artifacts allow users to travel from one spot to another within a dimension in the blink of an eye."

"Or from one dimension to another," Alice added, her expression dire. "But that takes a lot more out of the user than intra-dimensional travel."

I thought about what they'd told me for a moment, remembering the unexplained robberies Grym had mentioned. "Could it be used to step inside a bank vault, for example, and steal everything inside?"

"Precisely," Alice said, looking a little gray. "If Detective Grym finds out we have it, we'll be in for a real bollocking."

I had no idea what that was, but it didn't sound good. "He can't blame us that the suitcase ended up at Croakies."

Sebille's gaze locked onto Alice's, causing the Keeper to flinch. "No. But he can certainly blame you for not knowing what it was immediately and locking it down properly," Sebille said in a quiet voice.

Alice got up so suddenly that her chair toppled backward. She walked away from it, toward the tea counter, and began making herself another cup of tea as if she hadn't just been called out by the sprite.

Unless you counted the stiff and jerky way she performed the task.

I gave Sebille my best *holy humperdink* look and she nodded.

Alice was a bit calmer when she returned to the table. "I'll contact the Universal governing body today and offer my resignation."

Silence throbbed between us. I looked from one to the other of the two women. Something big had just happened, and I'd somehow missed it. I lifted my brows at Sebille, willing her to fix whatever it was.

She rolled her eyes. "I doubt that's necessary," she told Alice. "But you should tell them about the situation. They might have an idea of how to deal with it."

Alice nodded but didn't speak.

Finally, Sebille stood up. "I'll go." She threw me a look and then headed for the door.

Since Alice didn't say anything, I spoke up. "Thanks for your help, Sebille. And for...fixing...me this morning."

She inclined her head, skimmed a final glance at Alice, and left.

Alice dropped her head into her hands. She looked utterly miserable.

I struggled with whether I should just quietly leave, give her some privacy and time to pull herself together, or try to smooth things over.

I opted for the latter because...well, to be honest, I was still curious about it all. "Don't worry, Alice, it'll all work out."

She said nothing, her head still in her hands.

I tried again. "You shouldn't let Sebille's opinion get to you. She's just one sprite after all." I chewed my bottom lip, feeling like I was talking to myself.

Alice's head snapped up. "Just one sprite?" she all but shrieked at me.

I flinched, suddenly realizing I should have gone with my first instinct and escaped to my little hidey-hole.

"Just *one* sprite," she repeated as if she couldn't believe how stupid I was. "That's just brilliant."

Judging by her tone of voice, I was pretty sure that word didn't mean what I thought it meant. I should have kept my mouth shut. "I'm...sorry?" I said, not exactly sure what I was sorry about.

Alice laughed a bit hysterically. "Just my luck we'd run into her on the street. Just my bloody luck."

I was starting to suspect that maybe Sebille was not what I thought she was either. "Who is she?"

Alice took a deep breath and let it out in a long, unsteady breath. "Only the princess of the bloody fae in Enchanted," Alice said angrily. "That's all."

15

NOW WE'RE GETTING TO THE MEAT
OF IT

I busied myself all day selling books and taking care of bookstore business. Alice had taken herself up to her room not long after Sebille left, pleading a headache. I'd heard her yelling at someone shortly afterward and figured she'd called her superiors as she'd said she was going to do.

I was half afraid she'd come marching through the dividing door any minute with a packed suitcase and announce that she was leaving.

The thought made my armpits sweat and stars burst before my eyes.

Down by my feet, Fenwald made a small sound of concern and I glanced down at him, getting a tentative paw to the thigh in question.

"I'm fine, Fenny. Just feeling a little insecure. You're not going anywhere anytime soon, are you?"

The big cat gave me a throaty yowl and rubbed

against my leg, wrapping his enormous form around both of my calves before heading for a bright square of afternoon sunshine for a nap and a bath. It was his usual routine and nothing seemed to interfere with it.

I smiled as he flopped heavily onto the carpet and rolled onto his back, all four long legs beating the air as he batted at dust motes dancing in a sunbeam.

If only my life were as simple as Fenwald's.

The bell jangled on the front door and Lea walked inside. She smiled at me. "How's it going, Naida?"

I briefly considered telling her about the possible legal kerfuffle with the suitcase, but decided that would be disloyal to Alice. The poor woman needed someone on her side in the current mess. "Busy and terrifying." I grinned to lighten my comment.

"Terrifying? What's going on?"

I quickly told her about our adventure at Gnomish the night before.

By the time I finished, her face was filled with concern. "Gnomes can be really dangerous, Naida. You shouldn't mess with them." She cocked her head. "You're lucky you got out of there alive."

"We were lucky to have Sebille along," I said.

Lea grimaced slightly and then quickly smoothed her features, nodding.

"What?"

"Nothing."

"No, really, Lea. Tell me. I'm feeling my way along here. If you can shine some light on anything...anything at all...it would be a huge help."

Lea crossed her arms over her chest and seemed to be carefully considering her words. Finally, she said. "She's just not my favorite person."

"Sebille? Why?"

"I find her a bit..." As she struggled with the right word, my mind surprised me by filling in a few that were less than flattering.

"Bossy?" I suggested.

Lea's brows rose and she nodded. "That could work."

"Condescending?"

"Yes, yes, that one fits nicely."

"Judgmental?"

"Now we're getting to the meat of it," Lea said in an "atta boy" tone of voice.

I grinned. "She's a bit hard to take. But she saved our lives at Gnomish, and she healed me this morning. She didn't have to do any of that."

Lea got a strange look on her face. "Didn't she?"

"What are you implying?"

The dividing door opened and Alice walked into the store holding the dreaded suitcase. She blinked in surprise when she saw Lea. "Oh. Hullo, sweetums."

"Hey, Alice. How are you?"

"Aces." Alice's smile seemed forced.

I glanced at the suitcase artifact, alarmed to see it in her hands. "Where are you going with that?"

The Keeper bristled at my question and then seemed to catch herself, giving me another strained smile. "I'm taking it to the PTB. It's too dangerous to leave here."

Lea was staring at the suitcase with a look of horror on her face.

"What's wrong?" I asked her.

She didn't seem to hear me. I reached out and touched her arm. "Lea?"

She blinked and turned to me. "What?"

"Is there something wrong with the suitcase?"

She shook her head, her body overtaken by a violent shudder. "The aura is..." She shuddered again.

"A red so deep it's almost black," Alice said, nodding. "Like blood."

"What does that mean?" I asked.

"Evil," they both said at once.

Awesome sauce.

"You should call Grym and ask him for protection while you travel with that thing," I told her, sudden worry tightening my chest.

"I'll be fine, Naida. But thank you for your concern, sweetums." She glanced toward the big cat stretched out in the fading sun. "I'm leaving Fenwald here. Do you think you can give him his dinner precisely at five?"

"Of course. Where are you meeting the PTB?" I asked.

"Enchanted Park, near the pavilion. I shouldn't be long." She headed for the door, her steps brisk. "Ta!"

As the door closed behind her, Lea turned worried eyes to me. "She shouldn't be alone out there with that thing."

As if to verify Lea's concern, Fenwald suddenly jumped up from his spot on the rug and ran to the front door, yowling and hissing in obvious feline hysteria.

Lea's words confirmed what I'd been thinking. "Should we call Grym?"

She shook her head. "The PTB are anonymous by choice and necessity, Naida. The Universe wouldn't thank us for bringing the Enchanted Police into this."

"Then what?" I asked.

She thought about it for a moment and then grabbed my arm. "Lock up the store. I'll meet you out front in five minutes."

Lea's car wasn't really a car. She drove one of those baby trucks that were only good for carrying small stuff in the truck bed and barely big enough for two people in the front. On the positive side, it was bumble-bee yellow.

As I climbed into the cab, I gave Lea a raised eyebrow look.

"What?" she asked defensively.

"This thing glows in the dark. It's not exactly conducive to following discreetly."

She grinned. "I put a cloaking spell on it. It will kick in every time we get within two blocks of Alice's car."

I looked around the small but comfortable cab. "This is cute."

Lea's grin widened. "I love my Bee. I carry a lot of plants and supplies in it."

"Yeah, I can see how you could get a couple of geraniums and a really small flower pot back there."

"Har!" she said, her lips twitching. "You'd be surprised by how much this little truck holds."

We headed for the park, Lea driving faster than she should because we needed to catch up to Alice. Fortunately, the Keeper drove like an elderly man, slow and a bit wobbly since she was generally looking everywhere but at the road.

We finally spotted Alice up ahead, her car weaving from side to side like she was drunk.

"Does she always drive that way?" Lea asked, her voice filled with concern.

"I'm not sure. I've only been in the car once with her. She does wobble around a bit when she drives. But I didn't think she was that bad."

The car slowed slightly as it came to the park entrance and then sped up again, zipping past the turn.

"What's she doing?" Lea asked, pressing her foot on the gas to catch up.

"Maybe she spotted us," I suggested.

"Not a chance," Lea said, shaking her head. "This cloaking spell is fool proof."

"Then she must have never intended to go to the park," I said, a feeling of dread oozing through me.

We followed Alice in silence for ten more minutes, my chest tightening with every passing mile because I was beginning to realize where she was going.

I didn't want to say anything until I was sure. If I was right, Alice wasn't playing for the right team. And my life was going to get exponentially more difficult if that was the case.

"What in the world?" Lea asked as Alice turned into the driveway of a well-known business.

My stomach twisted painfully at the realization that my suspicions had been right. "No, no, no. Alice, what are you doing?"

Lea parked the truck on the street, half a block

from the entrance to Gnomish, Inc. and under a tree so the silvery glow of a quickly rising moon wouldn't highlight its presence there.

I slumped in my seat, silent and miserable.

Lea's gaze scoured me. "What's going on, Naida?"

I turned a miserable gaze to her. "I wish I knew. But it doesn't look good."

"Do you think Alice is working with them?"

I shrugged, chewing my bottom lip as I tried to consider all the possibilities. "Maybe they threatened her again," I said. "It's the only thing I can think of that might make her do this."

"This is bad, Naida," Lea said softly.

"I know."

"Maybe it's time to call the police."

I realized she was right. It was highly doubtful Alice was meeting a PTB as she'd said. And if she was giving a dangerous artifact to the bad guys...

I sighed. "If we call the police, they'll arrest her."

"Yes." Lea's tone was gentle, as if she realized what the current mess was going to cost me and understood my reluctance. But it would be selfish of me to think about that. The cost to Enchanted and potential future victims was more important than my worry about a job.

"Okay," I finally said. "Let's call Grym."

Lea grabbed her phone from the cubby between the two seats and started to dial. I watched Alice go into the building and felt sick to my stomach. "How could you?" I murmured softly.

Something moved beyond the lights at the front of the building.

A shadow shifted.

I turned to watch as a slim figure slid from the shadows and stood staring up at the building. And then disappeared in a burst of soft green light.

I reached over and put my hand over Lea's. "Hang up."

She gave me a look that was tinged in impatience. "Naida..."

I shook my head, pulling her phone from her fingers and stabbing the button to disconnect. I handed it back to her. "We can't call Grym." I opened the door and started to climb out. She grabbed my arm.

"What are you talking about. We can't go in there. It's too dangerous. It's going to be everyone against us."

I gently disengaged myself from her grip. "You're right, you should stay here. If I don't come out in twenty minutes, then you can call Grym."

"Naida!" She made an outraged sound as I slammed the door on her concern.

Lea climbed out of the truck and ran after me. "Why can't we call the police?"

"Because I don't want to get Sebille in trouble."

"Sebille?" Lea frowned in confusion. "Why

would she get into tro..." A lightbulb went on behind Lea's pretty turquoise gaze. "Ah. What in the goddesses favorite Spanx is going on here?"

"I have no idea. But I'm about to find out."

I stopped and grabbed her hand. "I meant what I said. You should stay here. There's no point in both of us getting bludgeoned by gnomes."

"As reasonable as that sounds," she said, her expression wry, "I can help. I *want* to help."

I didn't have time to argue, so I nodded and took off running, Lea hot on my heels.

16

YOU ARE IN VIOLATION OF THE
QUEEN'S DIRECTIVES

I realized as we hurried toward the front door that we were going to be in trouble if the door was locked. Sebille was inside already and didn't know we were there, so she couldn't let us in.

I glanced toward the parking lot and it was empty except for Alice's car.

So, who was Alice meeting?

The whole thing was just a mess. I was terrified that, when I found the answers, I wasn't going to like them any better than the questions.

We tried the door and it was, of course, locked.

How had Alice gotten in? Had someone let her in? Or did she have a key?

My head was starting to hurt from all the questions.

Lea touched my arm, leaning close as she pulled me away from the door. "I can get us inside," she said in a whisper. "But I suggest we look for a back door. We don't want to stumble face-first into whatever's going on in there."

A grand suggestion.

I nodded, following her around the building in search of a less conspicuous entrance.

We found one half-way down the first side. The building seemed empty, all the windows dark, but I couldn't shake the feeling of eyes on our every movement.

Her hand on the doorknob, Lea's voice rose and fell in a low, rhythmic chant, sending a stream of magic into the lock. A beat later, it clicked open. We moved quickly inside, finding ourselves in an unlit back hallway that appeared to only service a water fountain and two restrooms.

We moved quickly down the short hall and jolted to a stop when we realized it fed directly into the lobby.

A voice echoed through the open space. Alice sounded as if she was about fifteen yards away, but it was hard to understand her because of the echoing effect.

We stood just inside the hall, pressed against the wall and listening carefully. When Alice stopped talking, no one responded for a long moment.

Then I heard a low, rumbly sound that might have been a voice.

Or it could have been my stomach complaining that it was empty.

Judging by the glare Lea was throwing me, I was pretty sure it was the latter.

I placed a hand over my stomach as if that would stop its grumbling, and eyed the immediate area beyond our hidey-hole.

The tree wasn't too far away. Its dense trunk blocked our view of Alice, but I was judging from the sound of her voice that she wasn't far from the front door.

I thought of the line of wooden gnome soldiers in that area and felt the blood rush out of my face. Alone against that army, Alice wouldn't have a chance.

Unless Sebille decided to help her.

I thought about that for a minute and realized they could be working together. Maybe Sebille was backing Alice up on some kind of sting.

But then, why hadn't they included me? Anger sifted through me and away. I'd certainly earned the right to be included. But the memory of the beat-down I'd gotten from the gnomes the last time made it hard for me to seek out that kind of "adventure" again.

Yet, there I stood.

"We need to get closer," Lea whispered.

I nodded in agreement and we carefully moved out of the hallway, stepping quietly to a spot behind the green space. Using the wide umbrella of the massive tree as cover, we crouched in the shadow of its branches and watched in surprise as Alice, standing in the middle of the entrance lobby, suitcase still in hand, spoke to the wooden soldiers lined up along the wall.

They stood as they had before, eyes dull and lips curved in smiles that seemed even more malevolent than the last time. I suffered a full-body shiver that made my teeth clack together from the memory.

"...poisoned the magic with her mark," Alice was saying. "I've been trying to fix it, but I need her to do it, and she's resisting my influence."

I frowned at the words coming out of the Keeper's mouth. Who was the *she* Alice was talking about? I thought she'd been the one to mark the suitcase and stop it from working.

Alice seemed to be listening to something, although I couldn't hear anyone else speaking.

"I know we had a deal..." she said, looking nervous.

My stomach twisted. My worst fears realized. Alice had been working with the gnomes. But then, if that was true, why had she hurt Gido?

"I'm doing everything I can. You need to give me more time..." she said, a pleading note in her voice.

I eyed the row of gnomes, wondering who Alice was speaking to. But I couldn't discern any movement or indication that any of them were alive.

They all looked exactly the same.

All had rounded forms. All were carved with coats that were painted blue and trousers that were painted a golden brown. All had clunky black boots carved on their feet, and all wore conical hats that were a dull, weathered burgundy color.

Every face had beady black eyes, a bulbous nose, and a sharp chin.

Alice suddenly lifted her head and looked toward the tree.

We hunched lower as her shadowed face stared in our direction.

I was afraid to move. But I was aware of Lea chanting softly beside me. I would have loved to ask her what she was doing, but I didn't dare make a sound.

"What is it?" a deep, gravelly voice asked.

The sound of it made me jump in surprise. But Lea looked pleased.

Alice turned her gaze back to the line of gnomes, lifting it above their heads. "I thought I heard something," Alice said.

The shadow on the wall behind the gnomes shifted slightly.

I reached over and clamped my hand over Lea's. She stopped chanting, her gaze sharpening on the lobby.

The gnomes began to move and my heart started to pound with dread.

Then   something   amazing...and horrifying...happened.

The wall shifted forward, peeling away from the shadows and forming into a gnome that looked a lot like the one in the office we'd searched the night before.

Only it was ten feet tall if it was an inch.

The enormous gnome had blended into the shadows, giving the impression of being part of the wall. How was that possible?

"Cloaking spell," Lea whispered as if answering my unspoken question. "I've been sending an interference spell into it."

The gnome was not only enormous compared to the wooden soldiers arrayed around his feet, but he was also not a minion. His tall form was leaner than the others, and it was covered in a dark suit with a white shirt and red power tie. The gnome's head wore no conical hat, and his hair was pure white, thick and wavy around a face that was all craggy planes and chiseled lines. He had a long, carefully trimmed beard that fell to a point below the knot of his tie, shaggy brows, also pure white, and a thick mustache that fell over the corners of his mouth to mingle with the beard.

Most importantly, I'd seen him before. I knew who it was.

Lea turned to me. "We're in trouble."

Aaaannnnddd, my heart redoubled its efforts to

claw its way out of my chest. In fact, it was beating so hard, I barely noticed the buzzing of a large insect as it flew past my ear.

But I definitely noticed when the bug stopped its flight in midair and hovered between us and the giant gnome, hands on hips and a glare on its tiny face.

Sebille!

The giant gnome glared down at the sprite, his hostile gaze over-scored by twin slashes of angry white brows. "Princess Sebille, what are you doing here?"

"Gerrard Gnomish the First, you are in violation of the Queen's directives. I've been sent to warn you to cease your activities immediately or face her wrath."

The gnome's angry eyebrows lowered even further over the beady black eyes. Gerrard Senior took another step forward, the weight of his tread making the branches above our heads tremble. The wooden soldiers spun out of his way, scattering in all directions to keep from being crushed. "You overstep yourself, Princess," the giant gnome ground out. "You are not your mother's enforcer."

Sebille's wings buzzed faster, sending her a few feet higher into the air. "You're right," she said, "I am not an enforcer. I am simply carrying a message from her. If you refuse to acquiesce to the warning, she will be forced to descend on Gnomish with an army of the fae."

Gerrard's wide forehead creased between his eyes. "To what purpose?" he growled out.

That seemed pretty obvious to me. Which made me wonder what he was up to.

As if reading my mind again, Lea said, "He's stalling."

I nodded, wondering if Sebille was aware.

She seemed pretty savvy, and she'd definitely been around supernormals longer than I had. But I just didn't know.

I glanced at Lea. "If you were working on something to help us get out of here, you might want to step it up a bit."

Lea nodded. "I need to grab a piece of this tree..."

I moved to the side, out of the view of the three in the lobby, and leaned over the short wall that encompassed the green space. Squinting through the darkness, I located what I'd been looking for streaming down the trunk in messy lines. My fingers grasped a thin but sturdy vine and tugged, extracting a portion that was long enough to reach Lea. "I don't know how all this works," I told Lea, "...but Sebille magicked these. Would there still be magic inside them?"

Lea nodded, her eyes taking on an excited glow. "This is perfect. I just need a couple of minutes to concentrate."

I nodded and moved away, my thoughts on that suitcase. I noticed that Alice had dropped it to the floor and was watching Sebille with obvious suspicion, her hands lifted and energy encompassing them in a charcoal gray glow.

I frowned. That didn't look right. Alice's magic was the color of mine. A pale silver.

Then I concentrated, tugging on the magic hiding in my core, and let it seep through me, giving me the power to envision Alice's aura.

I blinked in horror at what I saw. Pure black energy swirled around her, oily in its blackness and unusually intense, as if gathering for an attack.

Spikes of it speared from her fingers and lashed the floor beneath her feet.

Alice was building magic. And I was afraid I knew what she intended to do with it.

I glanced at Lea, finding her sitting cross-legged on the floor inside a circle she'd made with chalk. The vine was laying across her two palms and it was glowing, the energy slowly crawling up the climber and moving toward the tree.

It was going to take her a few minutes to do anything useful.

I needed a distraction.

But to do what I needed to do, I also needed an infusion of energy.

Closing my eyes, I pictured the magic coiling in my core and concentrated on building it. I pulled energy from my cells, propelling it into my core in an effort to create pressure. When I reached the end of my internal magical stores, I sent questing fingers of energy into the air around me, finding it a rich source of more magic and pulling it close. That was much harder. I hadn't learned to extract energy from the air around me. I'd barely learned how to pull it from my own stores.

But dire circumstances called for drastic measures.

Vaguely aware of the voices on the other side of the tree, I reached for the green space, finding pockets of Sebille's residual magic nestled among the flowers and bushes there. I carefully extracted the magic where it was willing to be collected, and gave up on the stuff that clung too closely to the plants.

I didn't have the strength or the time to force that magic to me.

When I felt as if my skin was tighter for the buildup of internal energy, I opened my eyes and sent my consciousness across the room, fixing it on the suitcase Alice had abandoned.

The energy left my palms in a thick wash, rather than the tidy ribbons Alice was able to expel.

My magic shot past the tree, sending its branches into motion like an errant breeze, and hit the suit-case with a whoosh. The suitcase wobbled a moment and then toppled to the ground with a loud thump. The sound was ominous in the magic-drenched air and I flinched, ducking as Alice's gaze shot to where I stood.

A rictus of a smile curved on her homely face, and for the first time I noticed she wasn't wearing her glasses. That surprised me because I didn't think she could see without them. She shoved her hands outward, palms facing me, and expelled a dense arrow of oily black magic toward my hiding spot.

It shot toward me like a cannonball and smashed into the tree, slicing off a good-sized branch and sending a cascade of deadly debris down on my head.

Somehow I managed to avoid any serious damage. And when I looked up, there was a glossy umbrella hanging on the air above my head.

My gaze skimmed to Lea. Her eyes were open and she was smiling, a dense spider web of magic written on the air before her, and her fingers twisted into the ends.

She'd given me a protective shield.

I sent her a thumbs up and her smile widened.

I didn't know how long the shield would last, but I intended to do what I could while it was there.

I turned back to Alice, who was striding my way with more ugly black energy boiling at her fingertips. Without thinking about what I was doing, I threw out my palms as she had and sent another wave of silvery magic in her direction.

The magic washed over her, blowing her frizzy brown hair off her face and pinning her plain black skirt against her legs. The magic left her untouched. But then it was supposed to.

A Keeper's magic wasn't defensive in origin. It was meant for calling magical artifacts into its grasp.

Strangely, however, I thought her curly hair looked a little...corkscrewed. Hm.

The suitcase lifted off the floor and hung there a moment, wavering on an invisible stream of energy. For a terror-filled moment, I thought it was going to resist me. Then, with a resounding chime that turned the gnomes' heads toward the elusive artifact, it shot straight up into the air and headed for me.

17

BY THE GODDESS'S RATTY TOILET BOWL BRUSH!

I reached a hand into the air and the suitcase smacked into it, wrenching my shoulder painfully from the impact and then dropping to the ground at my feet.

Or, more accurately, *on* my feet. It hurt like a mother bear. With a yelp of pain, I grabbed my foot and started hopping around, as if that would help it feel better.

The gnomes charged with a roar, the terrifying thunder of their heavy feet sounding like a herd of fleeing buffalo in the echoing space.

Lea surged upright, screaming Sebille's name in warning, and then shouted, "*Diffusis!*" and released the spell she'd woven on the air. It clung to her long fingers for a beat and then snapped backward like a web of rubber bands, smacking into the tree with a "whomp!" of energy that made the branches fold into the trunk for a beat and then blow outward, sending a tsunami of energy shooting across the space.

One by one, the gnomes toppled beneath the impact as it hit them, crashing to the floor and agitating there like turtles turned upside down, unable to get up.

I lost track of Sebille, but I had to assume Lea's warning had been enough for the sprite to gather up Alice and get them both to safety.

I had bigger problems to worry about.

Lea's spell managed to take all the wooden soldiers out of commission, but the big guy was still on his feet.

And he looked peeved!

He threw back his head on a roar that rattled the glass in the windows and stomped in our direction, each footstep shaking the floor beneath our feet.

I glanced at Lea, expecting to find her looking terrified. But her eyes were closed and her fingers danced on the air, already mapping another spell.

Whatever she was cooking up, I was terrified it wouldn't happen in time.

I looked around for Sebille and discovered both her and Alice missing.

It was just me.

And a hacked off ten-foot-tall gnome.

Knobby gnome's knees! Everything I did just seemed to make things worse.

I forced myself to think. There had to be something I could do. I tried in vain to tug on my Keeper energy again. But, when I reached for it, nothing answered. There wasn't even the tiniest tug of power. Either I'd expelled it all, or I was too stressed out to use it.

Glancing down at the suitcase, I had a thought. Could I use it to get us out of there?

I touched the old-fashioned latches on the top, and electricity arced up and bit my fingers, making me squeak in pain and jump back.

"*Glacio!*" Lea screamed. Her fingers were bent, cupping the air in front of her. Green energy, smelling of fresh herbs and sweet flowers, curled from her hands and, instead of hitting like a wave as her last spell had, curled through the air and wound around the gnome's feet and legs. He swiped angrily at the magic, flinging out a hand with a growl.

Energy flew from his fingertips and hit the tree. Like Lea's magic, the garden gnome's power smelled sweet and herbal, formed from the energy of growing things. But it had a decidedly more violent effect. The tree jerked and shuddered, and then sent its branches toward the sky with a rumble that might have been a growl.

I grabbed the handle of the suitcase and started to retreat. Her eyes closed, Lea continued to send her latest spell across the room. Whatever it did, I hoped it would do it soon. The gnome was still moving toward us, although he seemed to be struggling to move his legs.

More importantly, he seemed to have awakened the tree.

And it hadn't woken up happy.

I watched in horror as it swung a branch toward Lea, hitting her hard enough to send her flying backward. She slammed into the ground on her butt and slid across the room, smacking up hard against the wall near the hallway where we'd entered.

A series of stout vines reached out and found me, wrapping me in a sinewy embrace that pinned my arms to my sides and yanked me back when I started to run. Unlike last time, the vines weren't gentle. They wound tightly around my body, squeezing hard enough to make my bones creak.

My eyes bulged in terror as the thick creepers headed toward my throat.

It wasn't hard to figure out how *that* was going to end. A branch slammed into my hand, and I dropped the suitcase on a scream of pain. I was pretty sure I'd felt bones cracking under the assault.

Gerrard Gnomish finally seemed to have ground to a halt. He stood with one foot partially lifted off the floor and his hand pointing toward the tree, locked in space. The dark eyes glittered with rage, and the lips beneath the mustaches were curled into a snarl.

He was one hacked off gnome. And I didn't want

to be around if he managed to shove free of Lea's spell.

The vines climbed inexorably upward, their grip on my chest tightening to the point where I could barely fill my lungs with air.

Panic clawed at me, drawing tears to my bulging eyes. Two very important things managed to push past the fear in my mind. One, I was going to die. And two, I was really and truly sick of gnomes.

A door slammed, and I heard footsteps running across the tile floor. My vision was dimming as lack of oxygen took its toll. I saw the blurry outline of a too-slender woman with fire-engine red hair running toward the tree. She slowed when she reached the giant gnome, staring up at him as if wondering how he'd become frozen. Or wondering how long he'd stay that way.

Behind me, Lea groaned. Something in my chest loosened as my fear for her at least eased.

The encompassing vines were so tight that they were tearing into my skin. It was like being wrapped in knives. Twining their way up my body, the vines had found my throat. It was only a matter of time.

I would soon be dead.

Sebille turned to look at the tree. For just a beat, my vision cleared. I saw confusion in her expression. Then her gaze slid higher and stopped. Her face seemed even paler than usual, making her freckles stand out like an army of ink spots on her face.

"Sebille," I ground out. The word came out sounding strangled, so soft I was sure she wouldn't hear it.

But she started to run, and the last thing I saw as she sped toward me, was her leaping into the air and turning tiny in a bright pop of light.

And then everything turned charcoal gray.

I cy hands slapped me hard across the cheek.

I grumbled at the assault, swiping at the air in front of my face and missing my assailant completely.

"Come on, Naida," a hostile voice said. "Stop lying around. We've got stuff to do."

I knew that voice. It was snotty and uncompromising and...

Slap!

...and about to belong to a dead person.

My eyes flashed open, and my hand snapped up to grip the icy weapon before it could strike me again. "Stop. That!" I ground out grumpily.

Sebille rolled her eyes. "Finally! I thought you were going to sleep all day."

At this point, I'd like to report that I was safe at home in my little hidey-hole at Croakies. Unfortunately, that would be a lie.

I still seemed to be lying on the floor at

Gnomish, so I couldn't have been unconscious for all that long. "How long was I out?" I asked, easing slowly to a seated position as my head throbbed like the bass in a hard rock band. I groaned, putting a hand over my eyes and resting my elbows on my knees.

"At least five minutes. Maybe longer," Sebille said crankily.

I stared at her, my mouth open. "Five minutes? You were beating me senseless over five minutes?"

Sebille stared back, completely unconcerned with my hostility.

I gave up trying to stare her down. It wasn't worth it. I hurt all over. "I really need to stop coming to this stupid place."

"I second that thought," another voice said. I turned to find Lea heading our way. She spared me a smile and then looked at the sprite. "We need to go. He's working through that spell pretty fast."

I shoved to my feet, suddenly filled with energy. "You don't have to ask me twice," I told her.

The three of us started toward the front door, keeping as much distance between us and the giant gnome as possible.

A loud creaking noise, followed by a whoosh of flower-scented air, was all the warning we got that our time was up.

"Run!" Lea yelled.

We took off, running for all we were worth

toward the exit. As we neared the receptionist's desk, sparks lit the air and a wooden soldier stepped from the shadows. Then another, and another, and way too many more.

We slammed to a stop, started to turn, and realized Gerrard flippin' Gnomish had broken clear of Lea's spell and was turning to face us, effectively cutting us off from our secondary exit option.

"Gnarled gnome knuckles!" I yelled. "I'm really sick of these guys."

We stood there for a beat, looking from the line of approaching soldiers, to the stalking giant behind us.

"What now?" I asked my partners in crime.

Sebille sighed. "Now, we go to Plan Z." She grabbed the suitcase from me and threw it on the ground.

"Hey!" I objected.

"Open it!" she demanded, looking at me.

"Wha...?"

She all but stamped her foot with impatience. "Hurry up, Naida, they're almost on us."

"But, I can't..."

"Use your Keeper magic," Lea said, her gaze skimming from one problem to the other and her fingers dancing in the creation of a spell she wouldn't have time to complete. "A Keeper marked it, so a Keeper should be able to open it."

I bit back the words pulsing on my tongue. I

didn't have enough energy left to do anything useful. And because I was such a failure, my friends and I were going to die. "I don't think..."

"Just do it!" Sebille screamed, sending a stream of energy into the line of oncoming gnomes. The power hit the first several soldiers and knocked them onto their wooden keisters, but the next several gnomes in line just filled in for them, and they kept coming.

Behind the growing line, regular bursts of sparking energy told me Gerrard was still making more soldiers.

If I didn't figure out a way to open that suitcase, it was game over.

I really had no choice. My entire body trembling with terror, I placed my palm over the suitcase and dug deep for my magic. To my surprise, it bubbled up in response to my searching energy, rising from my core as I wiggled my fingers and lifted my hand, feeling it flow up my arm and into my fingers. My digits lit with a hazy silvery glow just as the first gnome attacked.

"Naida!" Sebille screamed, her hands aglow with energy that couldn't knock the nasty little guys back fast enough.

I panicked and threw my energy toward the suitcase. It flew off the ground enmeshed in a thin veil of silver energy and twirled around three times before slamming back to the ground.

I expelled a frustrated breath. "I told you I couldn't..."

The suitcase popped open.

Oh...

The interior was a swirling black nothingness, interspersed with silvery strands of magic that formed a coil which narrowed as it moved from the rim of the bag to its center. "What is that?" I asked.

"Portal." Lea stepped closer, one leg lifted over the vortex. Her eyes met mine. "Croakies," she said. And then she was sucked down into the vortex and was gone.

Sebille had popped into her sprite form while I was opening the bag. Her magic seemed to have more power when she was in that form, and she'd managed to create some space between us and the oncoming hordes. She flew backward until she was inches away from me. Without glancing my way, she said. "Step into the bag and think of Croakies."

Behind us, a roar went up and the ground shook beneath massive, thundering footsteps.

We were out of time.

"I'm not leaving you..."

"You won't," she screamed, turning to blast Gerrard Gnomish with an energy bolt that knocked him back a few steps.

But not far enough. He regained his equilibrium in the space of a heartbeat and threw himself toward us, hand outstretched toward the open suitcase.

"Now!" Sebille screamed.

When I didn't move, she popped into full size, wrapped herself around me, and leaped into the hole in the suitcase.

The world went black and shimmery for a long moment, the sights and sounds of unidentifiable objects occasionally flashing past as the vortex carried us to our destination. Hopefully, Croakies, though I'd been so discombobulated, I forgot to think my destination as Sebille dragged me into the whirling miasma.

Without warning, our feet slammed into thin, dirty carpet and we stumbled forward, barely staying on our feet as momentum carried us away from where the portal had spit us out.

A heartbeat later, something slammed to the ground behind us.

I turned to find the suitcase lying on the carpet where Sebille and I had come through. It was closed again.

"By the Goddess's ratty toilet bowl brush," I groused, turning and sliding down the wall to my butt. "If I ever suggest that we go to Gnomish again, please hit me upside the head with something big and heavy until I'm in a coma."

Lea was sitting at the table in the center of the room, her head on her arms.

Sebille staggered over to the tea counter and started making tea.

Crazy sprite.

But I'd definitely have my hand in the air for a cuppa when it was done. Yes, I would. "What just happened?" I asked nobody in particular.

Lea groaned.

Sebille set the freshly filled teapot on the stove. "That wasn't Alice."

I'd figured that out, or at least considered it a possibility, but hearing the words was still startling. "Then who was it?"

"I'm not sure," Sebille said, "but I've been following her since yesterday, and at some point between her leaving here tonight and ending up at Gnomish, something changed."

I thought about what she'd said, remembering how Alice had been weaving around even more than usual on the drive over. And how she'd slowed at the entrance to Enchanted Park but hadn't turned. "Alice got into her car intending to take that suitcase to the PTB," I said.

Lea lifted her head, nodding. "I'm pretty sure that was her."

Sebille didn't respond. She busied herself with the tea things.

A thump rattled the dividing door. A long, angry yowl filled the room. I groaned, realizing I'd neglected to feed Fenwald. I got to my feet and shuffled to the door, already apologizing to the cat. "I know. I'm sorry..." When I opened the door, the big cat came flying out of the artifact library, but he didn't run to the tea area as he usually did, begging for food. He flew toward the front door instead, yowling and flinging himself against it as his tail snapped angrily behind him.

"Fenwald, what...?"

The door flew open, slamming against the wall behind it.

Lea surged to her feet, hands out in front of her and energy dancing over them.

Sebille popped into sprite form and raced toward the door.

I stood there with my mouth hanging open. Helpful as always.

Alice stumbled through the door, collapsing to the carpet in a limp puddle.

18

BEWARE THE IMPLEMENTS OF TRAVEL, FOR THEY OFT BE DEADLY

"I've never seen him before in my life," Alice said.

We were all in her apartment, watching her bite gamely into a two-day-old scone that had been like granite when it had first been baked and had to be like biting into a diamond after two days. However, I noticed she'd soaked it in her tea for a couple of minutes before biting down on it.

Somehow the rock-like pastry gave way under her teeth with a brittle sounding crunch. Those suckers had to be like T-Rex choppers.

Sebille eyed Alice with an expression filled with doubt. "You say he was in your car when you got inside?"

Alice nodded, chewing as if she had four inches of leather between her teeth.

"What did he look like," Sebille asked.

The keeper shrugged. "No idea. He must have given me a Forget spell."

The way Sebille's gaze was narrowed, I got the impression she wasn't buying it.

"I don't understand why he didn't just take the suitcase and go," I said. Nothing that had happened to that point made any sense. And it was giving me a headache. "Why'd he use a spell to look like Alice?"

Alice swallowed, sipping tea to flood the rigid combination of flour and butter down her throat. "Before he knocked me insensate, he said something about me and my merry band of idiots..." She gave us an apologetic look. "...getting in his way. And then he declared that he'd make sure nobody listened to us if it came to that. He likely took my form so anybody who saw me going into Gnomish would think I'd given the suitcase to Gnomish, leaving him in the clear."

"From what we heard, he obviously had an agreement with Gerrard," Sebille said. "And the gnome isn't happy that he can't use his new toy. Heads are going to start rolling if the gnome doesn't get a working suitcase back soon. And the wizard knows his head will be first on the block."

We chewed on that while Alice risked another bite of lemon-flavored diamond.

"What kind of spell was that?" Sebille asked.

Lea glanced at the sprite. "He used a doppelganger spell. I could see the fractured aura, but I wasn't sure, at first, what it was. I've never seen one firsthand before."

Sebille frowned. "Are you sure it wasn't a four-dimensional glamour?"

Shaking her head, Lea said, "No, a glamour doesn't noticeably change the aura. It sits on top of a person's form like a full-body mask." She held her hands up, curving her fingers and sliding them together. "A doppelganger spell inserts jagged edges into the person's aura, fitting them together like parts of a puzzle. It's almost impossible to see unless you recognize the aura change."

Alice dunked her scone, the durable snack clinking against the edge of the mug like metal. "I woke up in the trunk of my car, disoriented and feeling weak." She lifted a haunted gaze to us. "Fortunately, I've been there before...don't ask...and was able to escape from the trunk and drive back here." She shook her head. "I don't think this guy is going to stop until he gets what he wants."

I agreed, and the thought made me shudder with dread.

"I don't mind telling you it's taken a bit of the stuffing out of me." Alice added. "I'm knackered."

Lea patted her shoulder. "We'll get out of here and let you rest."

"Don't worry," I told Alice. "I'll take care of things downstairs."

Alice nodded, but she seemed to already have

forgotten us. She'd set her tea, scone still resting in the cooling liquid, on her bedside table and laid back down. She was already snoring as we pulled the door to her apartment gently closed.

We didn't speak until we were back in the bookstore.

Sprawled along the wide window sill at the front of the store, Fenwald turned his head to us as we came into the store, giving us a soft meow as if asking how Alice was.

"She's resting," I told the big feline.

He made a soft little whirring sound and then commenced to cleaning his paws, his ratty form mirrored in the glass of the big front window as he bathed.

I looked at my friends. "Tea?"

Lea shook her head. "I need to get home. But thanks."

I nodded.

Still, nobody moved. Like Alice, we were all tired and more than a little concerned about what had happened. Clearly, someone meant us harm, and we were moving blindly through a shifting landscape with a deadly artifact at its center.

"I'm worried about that suitcase," I told my friends.

Sebille nodded. "Me too. Though I don't know where it would be safer than the toxic magic vault in the back."

"That's only safe if Alice doesn't take it out again," Lea said softly. We were all silent for a moment, each of us no doubt trying to decide how we felt about Lea's observation and the unspoken message behind it.

There were so many questions and so few answers.

Why had Alice suddenly decided to take the suitcase out of Croakies?

Had it just been a giant coincidence that the creature who'd imitated Alice at Gnomish had been waiting for her to leave the store with it?

What had that creature been doing, imitating Alice?

Had he known we would show up at Gnomish?

And, if so, why hadn't he taken steps to stop us?

I rubbed my temple, getting a headache from the never-ending questions.

"I'll keep an eye on the vault tonight," I told them. "My hidey-hole is between it and Alice."

Lea nodded, squeezed my shoulder, and turned toward the door. "Let's talk in the morning. Maybe after a good night's sleep, we'll have a better idea of what to do next."

"See you in the morning," I said, watching her leave.

Sebille stood in front of me, thoughtfully pursing her lips.

"What?" I asked her.

It took her a beat to swing her startling gaze to mine. She held my stare for a moment and then quietly said, "Alice can't do this job anymore. She's compromised."

My pulse picked up, adrenaline flooding my system. "What do you mean? You think she was involved in that mess at Gnomish?"

"Involved? Probably not," Sebille responded. "But she's grown careless. A Keeper of the Artifacts can't be careless, Naida. This job's too dangerous. I'm worried about the situation here."

I was worried too. About Alice's competence. And about her apparent disinterest in training me to do the job. "I'll pick her brain. Step up my training." I took a deep breath. "I'll work harder and faster to fill in the gaps."

Sebille's expression was filled with something that looked like pity. She nodded and turned away, leaving Croakies without another word.

I locked the physical deadbolt and engaged the magical lock using the spell Alice had taught me the very first day. Then I turned off the lights and went to stand in front of the window, my fingers digging into Fenwald's fur as I watched Sebille hurry across the street and into the dark alley next to the vapery. I assumed there was a staircase leading to the upper levels and her apartment.

Or else she just popped into a bug and buzzed up to an open window.

I sighed, so tired.

Beneath my gently probing fingers, Fenwald's long body vibrated under a throaty purr. He watched Sebille too, his gaze still locked on the spot where she'd disappeared into the shadows as I yawned widely and said goodnight.

To my surprise, the big cat didn't head for the dividing door with me. He apparently planned to spend the night in the bookstore.

No doubt dubbing himself the night watchman for the store.

Goddess knew we needed one.

Yawning widely enough to crack my jaw, I headed for the dividing door. I didn't quite make it. The bookstore phone rang as I was reaching for the handle. Groaning aloud, I glanced at the wild-eyed black cat clock on the wall above the sales counter.

Ten o'clock. Technically, I didn't have to answer the phone. The store had been closed for hours. But I felt as if letting it go to voicemail would be like shirking my duties. So I trudged over and answered, hoping whoever it was didn't want anything that required a lot of brainpower. "Croakies Bookstore."

"Hello..." There was a short pause, during which I contemplated whether the caller wanted me to return the greeting. I'd opened my mouth to do that when she said, "Is this the Keeper?"

My mouth slammed shut. I didn't quite know what to say to that. Only the magic-using community knew that title and where to find the KoA. But it seemed imprudent of me to just blurt out verification of it over the phone. "Who's calling, please?"

A sigh wafted through the line. "This is Maude Quilleran. I want to hire the Keeper to help me find an artifact. I know it's late, but I'm kind of desperate."

My thoughts tumbled over one another. It was clear the young woman...she sounded like she might be in her teens...knew of the Keeper and had a genuine need. I should turn her over to Alice. But Alice was resting and probably wouldn't want to speak to the teen. I could, of course, tell her that Alice would call her the next day. But then I thought of my conversation with Sebille. I'd promised I'd step up my efforts to learn, in case Alice fell short of expectations again. So I screwed up my courage. "Tell me what you need help with, Maude."

She made a happy little sound, and I couldn't help smiling. "Oh, thank you, thank you! I've been freaking out!"

Definitely a teen. If the youthful voice hadn't given her away, her tendency to speak in exclamation points definitely would have.

"What's going on?" I nudged.

"It's my hairbrush. It's spelled, of course."

Of course, I thought, smiling. Wasn't everyone's brush spelled?

"And Margo Collinsworth took it because she's

mean as a snake! I need to get it back because Margo's a muggle..." she giggled. "Sorry. I know that's not a real thing, but I just love that word, don't you?"

"Um..."

"Anyway, Margo the muggle took my hairbrush because she's jealous of my hair, and I don't want her to use it!"

I frowned, feeling underwhelmed by the opportunity she was offering me. On the plus side, it sounded as if it was well within my limited means to accomplish. "That doesn't sound too dire," I started to say.

"Did you miss the part where I said it was spelled?!"

Shoving away irritation at her slightly snippy tone, I decided I needed to net the problem out. "What is it spelled to do, Maude?"

"Give me lustrous, perfect hair, of course!"

Of course. "Okay, well, aside from losing the brush, that doesn't sound so bad."

"Did you miss the part where I said she was a muggle?!"

Okay. Got it. A muggle...erm...non-magic teen would probably notice a brush that gave her perfect hair. "And it would be obvious to her that it's spelled if she used it?"

"Duh! Margo's hair looks like the backside of a porcupine. When that brush touches it, she's suddenly going to have long, thick, shiny hair. The only way Margo could have hair that nice is if she wore a wig!"

Grinning at the "backside of a porcupine" reference, I said, "Got it. You want me to find the hairbrush?"

"Yes! Thank you! I'll see you there tomorrow at six in the morning!"

"Wait!" I yelled, realizing as I did that she'd infected me with exclamation points. "You'll see me *where*?"

"Oh..." More giggling. "At Enchanted High School."

Holy halibut halitosis! I was going back to high school.

19

BAGGY UNDERWEAR, MEAN GIRLS, AND MORTAL EMBARRASSMENT

To say my days in Enchanted High were difficult would be to seriously underplay the situation. As a supernormal with no discernible magic but a tendency to create unintentional havoc wherever I went because of my latent energies, I was a serious liability to myself.

I didn't really belong in the human world. And not belonging is about as mortal a sin in high school as one can commit.

But I also didn't belong in the magic world. Or, as I was informed by my non-magic grandma, I wasn't part of that world and it wasn't part of me.

So it should seem clear that I carried around a lot of emotional baggage in the form of self-loathing and feelings of inadequacy.

Looking back, I now realize that it made me pretty much a typical teen. But at the time, I'd thought I was queen gnish in a prickly and uncomfortable crowd of one.

Unlike teen-me, the young woman who strode quickly in my direction as I did a turtle walk toward the building was delicately pretty, confident, and sure of her place in the world.

Maude Quilleran smiled and waved, tossing a thick ribbon of wavy blonde locks over her shoulder as she fixed a wide blue gaze on me. "Hi! I'm Maude. You're the Keeper?"

I hunched into myself at her overloud proclamation. I was feeling like a fraud at the same time I was concerned over the young woman all but screaming my magical designation to the world at large. "In training, actually," I told her, taking her outstretched hand. "I'm Naida. The Keeper is under the weather." I assumed I was telling the young witch the truth, though I hadn't clapped eyes on Alice before I left Croakies at the buttcrack of dawn.

I assumed she was still blissfully asleep, cradled in the muscular arms of Morpheus. Whereas I'd been wrenched from an uneasy sleep by the strident shriek of an alarm clock and yanked into my worst nightmare by the icy fingers of fate.

Okay, drama much? Obviously, I was back in high school.

Maude nodded as if she didn't really care. She seemed to have an "any Keeper in a storm" attitude. The teen pointed toward the hated front doors of the large stone and brick building. "We need to hurry. Kids will start getting here soon."

Whether she realized it or not, her words were perfectly designed to turn me from the turtle to the hare. I launched from my spot on the rust-stained sidewalk like a rocket that was powered up to visit Mars. "Tell me about this brush," I asked as we hurried toward the large front doors. I had no idea what good that knowledge would do me, but I thought it would give me more gravitas as a Keeper if I pretended the process was deeply thought out and complex.

She shrugged, giving my question the weight it deserved. "Oh, you know, just a hairbrush."

So much for gravitas.

I tried again. "What color is it?"

She frowned, grabbing the front door and yanking it open. "Color? I guess I never noticed. It's kind of tree-colored, you know?"

Tree colored. Probably wood then. "Okay. Can you give me any more details?"

She ushered me through ahead of her and closed the door behind us, waving a hand over the wide, metal panic bars. She grinned when she saw me looking. "Just to slow them down a bit."

I panicked a tad when I realized she'd locked us into the building together. What if Maude was another persona created by the mage who'd done a doppelganger spell to look like Alice?

I decided I needed to do some kind of test to figure out if she was legit before I got in any deeper. Squinting my eyes, I tried to read her aura. I'd found, however, that if I tried to see auras I rarely could. Apparently, viewing auras is a natural phenomenon that resisted being nudged. At least for me.

She widened her already wide blue eyes at me. "Are you okay? You look a little...constipated."

"Ha!" I said. "Ha, ha."

The look on her face told me she was having her own doubts about being locked inside the building with me. "You're in training, you said?"

"Yes." I didn't elaborate because my elaboration wouldn't make her feel any better. Telling her I'd been on the job for less than a week was unlikely to comfort.

She shrugged again and pointed down a long, dark hallway to the right of the main doors. "Lockers are down there. I'm assuming that's where she put the brush."

We headed that way and I forced my mind to clear, taking a deep breath and slowly expelling it in an attempt to calm my nerves.

In the dim lighting, I could finally see that a soft glow painted the air around the young witch. Her aura was similar to Lea's, only with a tinge of gray that made me realize she wasn't an Earth witch like my neighbor. I made a mental note to do some research on witches. I was pretty sure that was some-thing which would make my job easier.

A sudden feeling of being overwhelmed swamped me and I had to take another breath as my heart started beating against my ribs. There was so much to learn, and I had the distinct feeling I didn't have much time to learn it.

Maude stopped in the center of the long hall, lifting her arms. "This is the best place to search." She cocked her gently illuminated head. "Should I try to find the lights?"

I shook my head, suddenly wondering what color my aura was. "I don't think that will be neces-sary." There was some safety lighting near the floor, and between that and the glow of her magic, I could see pretty well.

We stood there for a long moment. Maude shifted from foot to foot, her pretty leather boots an odd color under the greenish-gray illumination she gave off.

I felt her impatience like ants crawling over my skin.

My heart tried to beat its way out of my chest. It was the moment of truth.

I chewed my bottom lip.

Maude looked at her nails and then realized it was too dark to see them.

Something heavy slammed against the front doors.

Maude turned and looked in that direction, her body tensing.

"Hey! Is somebody in there? Can you unlock this door?"

I was well and truly out of time.

"Can you hurry?" Maude asked, tension threading her voice.

I flapped a hand in the direction of the door. "Head that way. I'll have the brush by the time you get there and you can unlock it."

I even shocked myself by the confidence strengthening my voice.

Maude nodded and turned away, her tall boots click-clacking down the hall.

I took a deep breath, wrung my hands, and pictured the core where my magic waited. At first, I didn't feel it churning there and I had a moment of panic that it hadn't replenished after the nightmare at Gnomish. Nightmares actually...

Energy began to stir deep within me. The magic felt warm and impatient. It churned and bubbled upward as my mind reached metaphysical fingers to entice it out of its hiding spot. The power oozed upward, threading through my cells and heading toward the surface of my skin. I realized that if I didn't find a way to focus it, the energy was going to blast away from me in a wall of power that might do more damage than good.

My pulse pounded and sweat beaded on my

forehead as I tried to redirect the magic into a single stream, slowly corralling it until it wound together in a thread that felt almost too frenetic to control.

I didn't bother trying to control it. I was running out of time. I let it flow upward, burning a path through the cells of my arm and surging toward my fingertips.

Another slam on the door made me lose focus. The magic halted and started to retreat.

No, no, no, no! I gritted my teeth and focused harder, forcing it to stop retreating.

"Naida?" Maude's high-pitched voice sounded more strident.

I couldn't respond, or I'd lose what I'd built. My body shook, and I realized I'd clenched every muscle in my body trying to hold onto the untrained magic. Still, it hovered, on the verge of retreating back to my core, unused. If I didn't get it out, I was going to lose it.

So I took a deep breath and forced everything to relax, and my mind formed a single word that slid from the depths of my consciousness.

Locate.

The word served as a focus for the power. It tore from my fingers on a hiss of displaced air, shooting toward the ceiling. Just before the energy smacked into the ceiling, it stopped, throbbing there for a couple of beats and then dissolving into several slender ribbons that dispersed along the hall and into the darker recesses of the big building.

More pounding shook the front door and several voices called out, sounding angrier by the moment.

"Naida!" Maude sounded frantic.

I glanced her way as the first chime sounded, relief flooding me. A second chime sounded a bit farther away. The sound of something whirling through the air brought my head up, and I reached for the item flying toward me. To my dismay, the object glanced off the heel of my hand and flew away. It hit a locker down the hall and landed in a clatter on the floor, skidding over the slick surface until it bumped against Maude's boot.

She looked down and gave a squeal.

I flinched, certain that scream meant I'd retrieved a dead mouse or something equally repugnant to a teenaged girl.

Like a history quiz.

But she reached down and scooped up a hairbrush, holding it in the air for me to see. "You're the best!" Then she waved her hand over the bars and shoved both hands into them to open the doors. "It must have been stuck," she said to a group of angry teens.

I felt the whisper-soft touch of something against my back. Reaching over my shoulders and around my back, I groped around as best I could but couldn't find anything. It had probably just been a breeze from the opening doors.

The lights in the hallway flashed on and I started quickly forward, hoping I could slide through the doors without being seen by the crowd.

"Naida!" Maude called out as I tried to slip unseen past the roiling crowd of hormones and emotions.

Bear boogers! I'd almost made it.

Then somebody giggled.

Somebody else guffawed.

Hilarity exploded all around me.

My nightmare blossomed into real life. Everyone was tittering and pointing at my backside.

Or maybe it was at my mom jeans. Either way, I wanted to turn and run as fast as I could into the early morning freedom beyond the doors.

I whipped around, pressing my back to the door frame, my gaze searching frantically for a way out. But I was trapped.

Surrounded by a sea of laughing, mean-eyed teens, all focused on me.

It was every naked school dream ever dreamed, all tied up into one horrible, beyond-embarrassing moment.

Maude walked up and frowned, her gaze similarly fixed on my wide back end. "What in the world?" To my horror, she reached toward my bottom. "Naida, why do you have a pair of men's boxers attached to your backside?"

With every blood molecule in my body racing to my face, I snatched up the boxers and made a run for it, shoving my way through the cackling crowd like my mom jeans were on fire.

I'd made it to the street by the time Maude caught up to me.

I could be fast when I wanted to be, but she was apparently faster.

"Naida!"

I reluctantly turned, wishing she'd just let me slink miserably away. Her gaze slid to my hand, and I realized I was still holding the boxers. My cheeks burned even hotter. I hadn't thought that was possible. I reached behind me and opened the door of Alice's ugly sedan, flinging them inside. "Evidence," I said stupidly. I had no idea what they were evidence for unless someone wanted to prove the preference for boxers over briefs in the teen population.

She nodded, her face filled with understanding. "I wanted to thank you for finding my brush for me."

I nodded. "No problem. It's kind of my job."

"I want to pay you for your work."

I shook my head. "No need. I'm already paid to do this for people."

"Oh, who pays you?"

I opened my mouth and then closed it, having no

idea. "Um, I'm not at liberty to say?" That the statement ended in a question was unfortunate. But it just seemed to work anyway.

Maude gave me a quick hug. "I'm going to find some way to repay you," she said, and then took off running as the bell rang inside the school.

I sagged in weariness and relief. "I'm glad that's over," I murmured to myself. Then I climbed into the ugly sedan, plucked the boxers off the rearview mirror where they'd landed, and left Enchanted High in my dust.

20

BLESSED OBLIVION, TAKE ME AWAY!

I turned onto Arcane Avenue and headed slowly toward Croakies. The traffic was light at that time of the morning, most shops not opening until ten a.m. or later. I was tired. My bones weary and my eyes heavy, and I wondered if I could sneak in a little nap before I needed to open Croakies.

The thought made me smile. I was quickly becoming comfortable with the concept of being a store owner. Which was good, because one day, probably much sooner than I'd expected, I was going to own Croakies.

My stomach did a little flip at the thought. I was going to have my own business. Somehow, that fact had gotten lost amid the worry and challenges of the other side of Croakies. The Keeper of the Artifacts side.

But I loved books, and I loved the idea and practice of having a bookstore. I was pretty good at it, too. And I was making friends.

My weariness lifted at the realization that the last few days hadn't been a total loss. In fact, looking back at them, I realized that I'd felt more alive during the ten days since Agent A.P. had shown up at my grandma's home and told me that I was destined for a magical vocation, than I had the entire twenty-two years previous.

The constant, nagging unease that had tightened my belly and made it hard to breathe for the last several days suddenly loosened. I'd just performed my first solo artifact retrieval. Granted, it hadn't been complex or dangerous...except to my self-esteem... but it had been a real job. And I'd completed it. All. By. Myself.

I was full-on grinning when I turned my head at the sight of a slender man walking briskly down the street.

My eyes met his. His expression darkened. And I gave a little shriek as he took off running the opposite way down the street.

I yanked the steering wheel to the right and headed for the curb, slamming on the brakes as one front wheel hit the curb and slid off with a jarring bump. I turned the car off and jumped out, digging in and racing after the retreating man, who, unfortunately, was a block ahead of me.

My thoughts spun as I ran. I had no idea what I

was going to do if I caught him. But since I'd engaged the chase, my pride and a strong practical streak wouldn't let me give it up.

I'd found our killer. And goddess only knew when I'd find him again. My hand slid to the pocket of my jeans and found my phone. Unfortunately, I didn't dare take my eyes off him long enough to call Alice. I told myself I'd follow him to his destination...run him to ground...and then call for help.

It was a solid plan.

But, best-laid plans and all...

The man stopped in front of an empty storefront and flung out his hands, an oily black mist rising from each palm and spreading into a cloaking wall between us.

By the time I reached the dissipating magic barrier. There was nothing there except an oily black stain on the sidewalk.

My breath heaving in and out of my lungs, I glanced around for a possible hidey-hole. The stores were all closed, dark, and silent. There were no vehicles nearby that he could be hiding behind.

Had he created a vortex like he'd done at Croakies and slipped through it to escape? My admittedly rudimentary knowledge of vortex magic told me he'd have to have a destination in mind.

I wondered if there were a distance limit on that destination.

Disappointment rounding my shoulders, I

walked the remaining two blocks of Arcane Avenue and found no sign of our killer.

I turned and started back to the car. Five blocks up, the ugly Croakies sign swung gently on a warm breeze. I had a horrible thought. What if he'd been coming back from Croakies? What if he'd hurt Alice? Or Fenwald?

I picked up speed, starting to run again as possibility turned to certainty in my overstimulated brain.

I whipped past a dry cleaner's, the taco shop where Alice had gotten us dinner, and a travel agent. Alice's ugly sedan was parked a half-block ahead, its back end sticking too far into the street and its front tires turned at an impossible angle. The driver's side door was hanging open.

Oops. Not one of my better parking jobs.

I was so focused on getting to the car, I nearly missed it. In fact, my eyes skimmed over it and I was several strides past the store before my brain registered the fact that the door to the travel agency was unlatched.

I skidded to a stop and backtracked, peering through the window with my hands on either side of my eyes to block the bright morning sunshine. The place was dark and appeared empty of people. Movement deep inside caught my eye. I realized I was seeing just a sliver of an open door. And someone was moving around in there.

Maybe whoever it was had seen or spoken to my mystery wizard.

I shoved my phone back into my jeans pocket and pulled the door open, sticking my head inside. "Hello?" Silence met my greeting. I stepped inside. "Is anybody here?"

The office smelled of old coffee, slightly newer flowers, which I saw wilting in a vase on the desk, and something else I couldn't immediately identify. Something unpleasant.

I looked around the place, seeing a snack area along the back wall, a plain wooden desk in the center of the room, and a long bank of gray file cabinets against the sidewall. One of those water dispenser things burped softly beside the door, and a brightly-hued travel poster rustled gently in the draft caused by the heating vent in the ceiling above it. Depicting white sand and turquoise waters as far as the eye could see, the poster declared, "Freedom from responsibility" and urged the wistful traveler to "Visit the beautiful beaches of the Caribbean".

I thought that sounded like a wonderful idea. Though it seemed unlikely I was going to get that chance any time soon.

"Hello?" I tried again. "I just wanted to ask you a couple of quick questions."

Although I couldn't see anybody, the air around me felt tightly strung, as if something hung there waiting to ignite.

My nose twitched under the elusive scent I'd finally identified. Sulfur. Dark magic.

The door at the back of the store was closed. I was sure it had been open when I'd been peering through the glass. I took a step toward the door, not even sure I'd have the nerve to open it and verbally intrude on whoever was back there.

As I stood there, dithering, I noticed a black mist oozing across the floor in my direction. My pulse spiked and I stepped backward, keeping an eye on the sulfurous-smelling magic.

Uh, oh. I'd stumbled on my wizard. I turned around and started quickly toward the door. As I reached for the handle, the deadbolt in the exterior metal door snicked closed with a horrifying finality.

Beware the implements of travel, for they oft be deadly.

The thought played itself through my mind and I had a moment of clear understanding. Implements of travel, a.k.a. a travel agency.

Gulp!

I grabbed the deadbolt and tried to unlock it, but it wouldn't budge.

"You really should have minded your own business," a darkly pleasant voice said from behind me. I whipped around, pressing my back against the door.

He stood near the desk, though I hadn't heard him enter the room. He was pleasant enough looking, as well as familiar. I remembered his slicked-back black hair and angular features from Croakies. It was the man who'd created the vortex to retrieve the suitcase.

My eyes felt like they were in danger of bulging out of my head. "You're the wizard."

He nodded in agreement, though it hadn't been a question. "I'm afraid so. And you're a nobody with nose issues."

My fingers frantically trying to unlock the deadbolt behind me, I made an effort to look unconcerned. I was pretty sure I failed. "You *did* murder someone. It's kind of a big deal."

The wizard shrugged, his black eyes sparking with humor. "Those gnomes are becoming a nuisance."

"Why'd you kill Gido? Was he trying to shake you down for protection?" I asked.

The wizard stared at me for a long moment, and I thought he wasn't going to respond. But then he crossed his arms over his chest and dropped onto the edge of the desk, extending his long legs in front of him as if we were going to have a long chat. "Nah. The little guy knew better than to try that with me. I had some business with his boss."

I nodded. "Mr. Gnomish. Unfortunately, I met him."

The wizard's smile eased slowly across his face, making him look almost handsome. "I know. I saw. That didn't work out so well for you, did it?"

My lips curled in a sneer before I could stop them. I really didn't want to give him the satisfaction of knowing he'd hit the mark. Reforming the sneer into a smile, I said, "We came out of it all right."

He shrugged, ceding me the point. "Gnomish tried to undercut me on our deal. I don't like to be double-crossed."

"So, you stuffed his guy into the suitcase?"

The wizard actually looked insulted. "Please, give me credit for more finesse than that." He laughed. "The little gnish wanted the suitcase. So I gave it to him."

My pulse picked up at the thought of what the gnome must have gone through, dying alone and helpless inside that artifact. "That's a horrible way to die," I murmured before I could stop myself.

"Don't waste your sympathies on Gido, Keeper. He was a miserable creature. Besides, his death was quick. Gnomes heads look hard, but they are actually fragile. It seems that falling the distance of the ceiling to the floor was enough to kill the little guy." He shrugged. "I'd actually hoped to get him to admit who sent him to shake me down before I killed him. He put a crimp in my plan."

"Who sent him? You don't know?"

"Oh, I know. I just wanted to get it on tape so I could take it to the cops if the gnome didn't back down. Gnomish isn't nearly as smart as he thinks he is. If he wants to undercut me, he needs to be much cleverer than sending one of his thugs in to try to steal the goods."

"What kind of deal did you make," I asked, my hands still working the lock. I needed to find another way out of there because I was quickly losing hope I'd get out through the front door.

"You've experienced the suitcase's magic?"

I thought about the trip from Gnomish, Inc. to Croakies and shuddered before I could stop myself. "It's some kind of portal." Giving up on the lock, I shoved my hands into my pockets instead.

"Some kind, yes," he agreed. "It's designed to take you to the destination of your choice and back again. The destination is entered at the time of embarking and then disappears immediately after delivery so nobody can follow." He gave me a mean smile. "If you try really hard, I'm sure even you can see why a criminal enterprise like Gnomish, Inc. might want such a treasure."

"The robberies," I murmured.

The wizard nodded. "Just a few test runs to show the client the value of the artifact I was offering him. Gnomish was supposed to give me ten million dollars for that suitcase." His face darkened with anger. "But he tried to bypass that part of our deal."

He'd sent Gido to steal the suitcase from the wizard. Bad gnome. Bad, bad gnome. I shook my head. "So, you killed him, stuffed him into the suitcase, and then what?"

His brows arched in obvious surprise. "You can't fit the rest of the pieces into the puzzle? I have given you the edges and most of the middle."

Despite his reference to jigsaw puzzles, which I have absolutely zero talent for, I felt compelled to play our little tableau out to its climax. "You dropped the artifact where Alice...erm...the Keeper would be sure to discover it."

He nodded. "It was a perfect plan. I got rid of the body and kept the suitcase out of Gnomish's greasy clutches."

"Then why did you break into the library and steal it back?"

The wizard's lips turned up in a mean smile. "Well, I'd always planned to grab it back anyway. That suitcase is much too valuable to leave to you derfs. But then Gnomish made me an offer I couldn't refuse. I had to move up my timetable."

I shook my head. "How much?"

"Twenty million." He frowned. "Imagine my surprise when we discovered that you busybodies had put a hex on the suitcase so it wouldn't work. I had my hands full keeping the big guy from going to war with me on that." The wizard fixed me with a glare that turned my blood to ice.

"What did you expect when you gave it to a KoA? It was her job to protect it. And to protect innocents from its use."

"Aardvark cankles!" the wizard barked angrily. "That artifact is mine. It doesn't belong to you."

Shrugging, I bit my lip against the desire to repeat that he'd given it to us. Instead, I asked, "How did you get Alice to bring it out of the vault? I assume it was you who she was meeting, rather than the PTB like she thought?"

His lips quirked upward in a mean smile. "It happens our Alice was contemplating embarking on a very long vacation soon. She has a particular affection for the Caribbean. I was very happy to make those travel arrangements for her. I'm a full-service travel agent, you know. With, in Alice's case, a teensy tiny bonus service she wasn't expecting thrown in. All it took was a bit of a suggestion hex in her tea..."

Slug snot! Alice had walked right into the monster's lair and given him a direct line to the artifact. "As much good as it did. You lost it anyway," I said, my gaze sliding toward the door he'd emerged from, wondering if I could get out that way. Of course, I'd have to get past him first.

"I'd have gotten it back if it wasn't for the interference of that stupid sprite. She somehow saw through my doppelganger spell and it was all I could do to get out of there alive."

"The glasses," I said.

"What?"

"You weren't wearing Alice's glasses. She can't see anything without them. It was a dead giveaway."

He made an irritated sound. "But the good news is. You're going to get it back for me."

"Me?" Okay, that squeak in my voice was embarrassing. "I'm just a trainee. I have no idea..."

"You'd better get an idea fast, sorceress, or you're going to find out firsthand how Gido died."

A faint sound eased into the room from beyond the walls. A hopeful sound. At least it was hopeful for me. It was a decidedly less encouraging sound for the wizard. His features sharpened as the meaning of the shrill sirens singing their way toward us sank deep.

I smiled. That was the point I'd look back on as being my fatal mistake.

He didn't like my smile. He didn't like it at all.

A shadow fell over the wizard, a charcoal gray miasma that seemed to rise from the carpet beneath his feet and paint his immediate area in an obscuring haze. His form seemed to swell, the humanoid outline taking on an amorphous structure that pulsed with the rhythm of a sluggish heartbeat. From his waist down, the mist tightened into a slender column of oily energy and then seemed to shrink downward, transforming into a shiny puddle of black ooze on the carpet beneath where he'd been standing.

I pressed backward as the puddle grew and ate into the fibers of the thin carpet, sizzling as it spread in my direction.

As the wizard continued to transform into the acidic ooze, his expression turned mutinous. He opened his mouth and a series of guttural commands emerged. The magic shook the walls and sent framed pictures crashing to the floor, the glass fracturing into a million pieces.

The acidic puddle picked up speed, streaming directly toward my feet. I knew with sudden certainty that if it touched me, I was dead.

"Goodbye, Keeper," the wizard growled as the last of his form turned liquid and melted into the running river of oily black magic.

The magic sludge flowed inexorably in my direction, eating everything in its path.

The wizard's magic was Death, with its sulfurous stench and promise of agony.

I cast my gaze around me in desperation, seeing no way out. I turned and yanked on the door, screaming as it refused to budge. Acrid smoke filled the room, wafting ahead of the killing ooze. I succumbed to coughing so violent I had trouble breathing through it.

The oily river was mere inches from my shoes, and I had nowhere to go. I glanced toward the window. The sill might be big enough for me to stand on. Its height would buy me a few seconds, though I had no idea if it would be enough.

I shoved the water dispenser onto its side as the puddle began to surround my feet. The carpet burned away around me, the foul stench of its burning fibers choking me until I couldn't breathe.

The water hit the black discharge, turning to steam too fast. I stepped on top of the dispenser's base and leaped, praying I would land on the sill before the oily magic reached me. I managed to get one foot on the sill and my hands slammed against the window, cracking but not splintering it. My other foot slipped off, arrowing toward the boiling magic streaming across the floor. For a brief, terrifying moment, I thought for sure I was going to fall. But I somehow managed to grab hold of the window frame, my fingers white with the effort of keeping me upright.

Beyond the glass, the sirens squealed closer.

But not close enough.

The oily ooze had hit the trim along the bottom of the wall and was climbing upward, reaching for me with long, spidery fingers.

In pure desperation, I stomped on the streamers of ooze as they breached the sill. A fiery heat burned instantly through the bottom of my shoe, eating through the rubber and taking a bite out of the bottom of my foot.

The magic carved into my flesh, slicing, biting, burning. Agony was too mild a word for how that acidic magic felt against my skin.

I screamed, the desperate, tormented sound foreign to my ears. My screams drowned out the sound of the police cars screeching to a stop at the curb, lights flashing, and the sound of battering rams pummeling the door until it crashed open.

My throat raw, I croaked a warning to the police, fearing the rabid sludge would take them out as easily as it was preparing to kill me.

There were shouts. Followed by the sound of wings beating the air nearby. Big wings. Some kind of massive bird clutched the oily ooze in its beak, dripping streamers of the foul stuff toward the ground. There was a pain-filled scream, likely from the reforming wizard caught in the creature's beak, a prehistoric screech that sounded like a victory cry, and then a familiar voice yelling, "I've got her."

Well-muscled arms caught me as I fell, pulling me against the comforting wall of a firm chest. My head lolled against that chest, the rhythmical thump of a strong heart beating against my ear.

I sighed, finally giving in to the desire to let go. To escape the pain. And allowed blessed oblivion to carry me away.

21

SQUEAK!

A Phoenix shifter, I mused, still amazed. Who would have known there'd be such a creature in the Enchanted Police Department? The thing hadn't even batted an eye at the burning ooze as it plucked it from the ground and threatened to swallow it, scaring the wizard into resuming his non-oozy form.

Making myself a promise that I'd shake the shifter's hand one day, I nibbled on a piece of buttered toast and sipped my tea. Like everything else Alice cooked, both were just a tiny bit off, but my stomach roiled from the previous night's events and I needed something inside it.

After facing off with the wizard, whose name I'd since learned was Leeds Mathews, I was really second-guessing my career choice to become a Keeper.

Maybe I could become a regular old librarian, far away from all things magical.

I liked books. I liked them a lot. Especially paranormal romance books. Maybe I could become a librarian of only paranormal romance books.

I sighed, swallowing the buttery bite of under-toasted bread and wiping my greasy fingers on a cloth napkin. I hadn't even known Alice owned real cloth napkins.

That she'd used one for me seemed to imply that she was feeling guilty about something.

Setting the tray on the floor beside my bed, I lay back and closed my eyes, my mind too active, and my burned foot too sore to allow more sleep. I thought about the face-off with the wizard. It had been terrifying. But I'd come through it alive. I'd been no match for the oily black magic Leeds Mathews had thrown at me, but I'd used my wits, hitting the button to call Detective Grym as soon as I'd known I was in trouble. Thank the goddess he'd programmed his number into my phone. All it had taken was a blind stab on my Favorites screen when I'd realized I was in trouble. Yes, I'd been lucky that Favorites had been open when the phone went to sleep. But still...

Through the open call, Grym had heard Leeds admitting to the murder of Gido the gnome. He'd realized I was in trouble, and he'd come with the cavalry to help.

Alice told me I'd still been unconscious when Grym had carried me into Croakies, but that a quick visit from Doctor Whom had, in her words, "put me to rights".

I had to admit that, whatever the strange doctor had done, my burned foot looked much better. It still ached, but the skin had gone from charred to pink during the hours that I'd slept.

Grym had, of course, filled Alice in on everything. She'd scolded me half-heartedly for not calling her in to deal with Mathews. Secretly, however, I was pretty sure she was pleased that I hadn't. Her training style seemed to be comprised of flinging me into the deep end and hoping I learned to swim fast enough not to drown.

Footsteps plodded heavily through the artifact library, heading in my direction. I could tell from the speed and heaviness of the steps that it wasn't Alice. My traitorous mind fed me the hope that maybe it was Detective Grym. I frowned at the pleasure the thought gave me. He was grumpy and judgmental. Although he was really cute. I shoved the thought away and told myself I was just suffering from hero syndrome. He had, after all, scooped me into his arms and carried me to safety.

It had been a heady experience.

Or, it would have been if I hadn't been drooping like a dead carp at the time, probably drooling on his shirt. Still, I sat up straighter, wiping the sleeve of my tee-shirt across my mouth in case I had butter on my lips.

It wasn't Grym. But the form that emerged from between the artifact stacks surprised me.

Sebille knocked on the frame of a shelving unit and gave me an assessing look. Lifting a bright red eyebrow, she said, "What's with the hair? You look like you have a giant starfish sitting on your head."

My hand flew self-consciously to my head. I glared at her. "I've had a day. Have a little compassion."

She actually snorted at that. "Yeah, compassion's not really my thing."

I was sensing that. "What can I do for you, Princess Sebille," I asked in a cool tone.

She grimaced. "Don't call me that. I'm not a princess. I'm just Sebille."

"Okay, Sebille. The question still stands."

She wandered into my hidey-hole and looked around, eyeing the trunk that grandma told me had come from my mom. She picked up the paperback novel sitting on top and flipped through it, a brow lifting at its subject matter.

"Put that down," I said a bit defensively. "That's how I relax."

"I bet." Her brows danced in innuendo.

"Sebille, are you just here to annoy me? Or did you have a purpose?"

She put the book back where she'd found it and

turned to me, all indication of amusement gone. "I've come to offer my services."

I blinked. "For what?"

"As your assistant. You'll need one, both magically and practically. Alice will be leaving you on your own soon, and you've proven many times over the last few days that you're not ready."

Fear and guilt stabbed me in equal measure. Deep down, I knew she was right. But admitting it at that moment was beyond me. "I've done pretty well for my first week of training," I told her. "I've solved three cases and managed to survive several attempts on my life." All the blood left my face as I did the math on the attacks I'd endured. I could feel each and every droplet scurrying away on tiny, blood-droplet feet, afraid to stay and face the knowledge that I was in way over my head.

Sebille nodded. "On the surface, that sounds pretty good." She must have seen the rage on my face because she softened. "You've actually done pretty well, considering how little real training you've gotten. But my offer stands. If...when...you become a new Keeper with too few resources, I'd be grateful if you'd call me."

Okay, that offer was a bit more gracious. I narrowed my gaze on her. "Why?"

"Why what?"

"Why would you offer to help me? I'm sure you

have better things to do than hang around Croakies."

Something passed through Sebille's long, homely face. Something that made me sad. Though if pressed, I couldn't say why.

"I like books," she said. "And I know a lot about magic. It happens I'm in between projects right now. I think you and I could help each other."

And that sealed it for me. Because, beneath the insults and overly-confident manner, Sebille needed a friend. And maybe something important to do.

Goddess knew I needed her.

I nodded. "I'll let you know. But it might be a few months. Are you okay with waiting?"

Tension I hadn't even noticed before slid away from Sebille's face and she looked pleased. "I am. Besides," she said as she turned to go. "I don't think it's going to be as long as you think."

I joined Alice in the bookstore a couple of hours later, freshly showered and too antsy to lay around in bed any longer. She greeted me with a quick smile that didn't quite reach her eyes and then slid her gaze away, pointing to a stack of new books that needed to be added into the inventory.

I settled happily to the busywork, happy to deal, finally, with something that didn't put me at risk of being bludgeoned to death or melted by a puddle of evil wizard.

I shuddered violently at the thought.

At six o'clock, Alice locked the front door and turned the Open sign to Closed. She joined me at the table, where I'd just finished inputting the last stack of cozy cat mysteries into the inventory system. I closed the laptop with a sense of having accomplished something good for the day.

I glanced at Alice. "Calling it a day?"

She nodded.

"I'm just going to put these books on the shelves and then maybe call for pizza or something."

"Brilliant. I'll go pick it up if you'd like."

"That would be great."

But Alice didn't move. She sat there, staring at her twining fingers, clearly wanting to say something.

I decided to help her get started. "Is something wrong?"

She took a long breath and sighed it out. "Actually, there is. I'm leaving."

For just a beat, I sat there happily oblivious, my mind refusing to recognize the meaning behind the startling words.

But then it hit me, and I flinched back in shock. After the shock, terror slid in to take my breath right out of my lungs. "What?" I gasped. "You can't. I don't know what I'm doing." I hated the shrieking tenor of my voice, but I didn't seem able to stop it.

Alice raised her hands in a defensive posture as if my words were bullets. "Not right away, of course. I'll continue to train you for a bit."

I relaxed slightly, my heart easing back from doing the rhumba against my ribs. "Oh, that's good. Don't scare me like that." I laughed breathily, but Alice didn't join me.

She still looked miserable.

"How long is a bit?" I asked.

She looked to the side, her fingers purple from wrangling each other on the surface of the table. Her mouth opened and closed a couple of times before she finally turned to me, still not quite meeting my eyes. "A month. Two at most."

It wasn't enough time. Not nearly enough. But I'd known I'd need to shorten my learning curve. I'd just have to tighten it up a bit more. I thought about it for a long moment and then said, "I want Sebille to come work at Croakies, as soon as she wants to come."

Alice must have felt really guilty because she agreed immediately. "I think that's a brilliant idea." She looked a little relieved, I noticed. Which made me wonder if she even planned to teach me anything in the final months.

Silence squatted between us like an ugly frog until I finally broke it.

"Why are you leaving, Alice?"

She shrugged. "I was always going to leave, Naida. That's why you're here."

"Yes, but my apprenticeship was supposed to last a year. And you haven't taught me anything yet." I knew it was a mean thing to say to her. But it was unfortunately true. And I was angry that she was abandoning me.

She flinched at my words but shook her head. "That's not true. You've actually done quite well this first week. I believe you've learnt a lot."

"By floundering around out of control, yes."

"Not entirely. And you've made friends who can help you. Friends who seem to already...care for you." Her expression turned sad. "In just a few short days, you've surpassed me in that."

How sad. Alice felt as if she had no friends. "Is that why you want to leave?"

Her gaze shot to mine. She seemed surprised that I'd be so blunt. But she chewed her lip for a moment and then answered my question honestly. "Maybe in part. But I'm tired, Naida. I'm ninety years old. I've spent most of my life as Keeper of the artifacts. I want something more. I want to travel and have some fun."

I could certainly understand that, so I nodded. I was still irritated with her, but I understood. And she was right. I'd begun creating a support structure for myself. More importantly, I'd formed new relationships that I treasured. I was luckier than I'd realized.

At that moment, fear for my future turned to hope and anticipation. I could do the Keeper job. I'd *been* doing it. Yes, it had been ugly. But I'd get better. And I had friends to help me keep my head above water when I needed it.

I actually smiled. "It will be okay," I told her.

Alice's smile eased some of the worry from her face. "Yes. It's going to be brilliant." She slapped her hands on the table and stood. "Now then. You make that call, and I'll go pick up our dinner." She headed toward the dividing door. "I just need to tidy up a bit, feed Fenwald and Oliver, send out a few emails, and Bob's your Uncle."

Bob's your what? I asked myself. Then I shook it off and made the call to my favorite pizza place.

Twenty minutes later, as I was slipping the last of the new books into their proper spots on the shelving, Alice was heading out the front door to pick up dinner when she made an exclamation of surprise. "Oh! Hello, sweetums. I'm afraid we're closed."

A young, sweet voice I recognized said, "I need to see Naida."

I came around the shelves and emerged into the open space as Maude Quilleran stepped through the door, a plastic carrier clutched in her hand. "Hello, Naida," she said, grinning broadly.

I hurried forward, relieved to see her smiling. My

reaction when I'd heard her voice was panic, assuming something horrible had happened because of my clumsy, if ultimately successful, artifact retrieval. But she was the picture of happiness.

And her hair looked spectacular.

I tucked a bristly strand of my wavy brown hair behind my ear and wondered if she'd let me borrow her brush. "Hey," I said, smiling. "Is everything okay?"

"Everything's fine," she assured me. "I wanted to thank you again for getting my brush. If that derf Margo had used it and realized it was magical, my dad would have played Beethoven on my colon for getting him in trouble with the PTB."

Grimacing at the mental image she'd created, I laughed. "I'm happy I could help."

Maude glanced around the store, her expression filled with awe. "This place is really icy. He's going to love it here."

I looked around too, trying to see it through her eyes. She was right. The cozy little bookstore *was* wonderful. I suddenly realized how much I'd come to love it. It was starting to feel like home. "Thanks," I said, grinning. "Can I get you something? I don't know if we have any pop, but I can make tea."

She shook her head. "I can't stay. My dad's expecting me home. He goes ballistic if I'm even ten minutes late." She rolled her eyes, giving even Sebille a run for her money with her technique.

"Okay," I said, waiting for her to tell me why she was there.

Maude looked down at the carrier in her hand. "I know you said you didn't want me to pay you for helping..."

I shook my head. "It's okay, really. I was happy to help."

"Meow."

I blinked in surprise at the soft cry, my gaze locking onto the carrier. "Oh, did you get yourself a kitten?"

A tiny gray face appeared in the mesh of the door, startling orange-gold eyes sparking in the overhead light. "Meow!" the little thing demanded, clearly sick of being inside the carrier.

"He seems to be unhappy about being in that carrier," I said. "How about if I got him some cream?"

"That would be great," Maude said, settling the carrier onto the carpet. She dropped to her knees and opened the door as I moved to the tea area and opened the small refrigerator, pulling out the container of cream.

"Meow," the kitten declared as he padded into the nook with me, winding around my ankles as I poured cream into a small bowl and placed it on the floor. The purring commenced as he bent to slurp his snack. "He's adorable."

Maude nodded enthusiastically. "He's going to love this place. So many nooks and crannies."

My head jerked up to find her looking hopefully at me. "Please accept him as my gift to you, Naida."

There was more to her request than a simple desire to pay me back. I could tell from the earnest expression on her face, and something that looked like worry in her pretty blue eyes. It was really important to her that I take the kitten.

I scratched his tiny back and frowned as I felt bone. He was too skinny. And I noticed as I sat down next to him that he smelled.

As if reading my mind, she said, "You'd literally be saving him, Naida. He needs a home. Someone to love him."

The fuzzy baby licked the bowl clean and then climbed into my lap, his contented purr rumbling against my legs. He closed his startling eyes and fell immediately asleep. "I don't know..." I started to say.

"Please, Naida?"

The kitten rolled over in his sleep, belly up, and I found it impossible to resist the fuzzy tummy he exposed. I was toast and I knew it.

I looked up and she smiled, the tension leaving her face at something she saw in my expression. Maude clapped her hands. "Yay! The only thing I ask is that you let me visit him once in a while."

"Any time. I hope you will."

She hopped up and down a couple of times and

then glanced at her phone. "Yikes! I'm late. I have to go." She started running toward the door. "I'll see you soon!" And she was gone.

I sat with my new baby for several minutes, enjoying watching him sleep. He sure moved a lot when he was sleeping. Hopefully, that didn't mean he was going to be a handful.

The bell on the front door jangled, and Alice came in. I panicked, realizing I hadn't cleared the new house member with her. Then I straightened my spine. She was leaving, and Croakies was soon going to be mine. I had a right to bring Mr. Wicked into my home. I stilled. Mr. Wicked. The name had just popped into my brain.

But I liked it. Loved it, in fact.

I was laughing when Alice came around the corner holding the pizza box. She blinked owlishly behind her enormous glasses. "Oh, look at that. I leave you for a few minutes, and you get yourself a cat."

I opened my mouth to explain, but she smiled. Crouching down, she gave the kitten a scratch on his tiny belly with one fingernail. "He's adorable. Fenwald will be thrilled to have his own trainee."

I watched in amazement as she moved toward the table and started putting out the pizza things. "I got us salads too, I hope you don't mind."

I didn't mind at all. Clutching my kitten close, I

joined Alice at the table, feeling more certain of my future than I had in a very long time.

———

"I'll get you some food and litter from Fenwald's stuff," Alice told me later. It was getting late and we were sitting with full bellies, watching with amusement as the kitten put old Fenny through his paces. Alice had been right, the big cat seemed to be cherishing his role as mentor, even if he was severely underprepared for it.

I yawned widely, my jaw cracking. "I guess I'll go to bed then."

Alice nodded. "I'll bring that stuff over in a bit."

Nodding, I shuffled toward the dividing door. "Come on, Mr. Wicked." To my vast surprise, the kitten complied, bouncing over and batting at the laces on my shoes. "He doesn't look tired," I said, concerned.

Alice laughed. "Don't worry, kittens run until they collapse, but he'll have lots of room to run in the library."

She wasn't wrong there. I pulled the door open.

"Oh, I nearly forgot. I put your medicine from Doctor Whom on Shakespeare's desk."

All my weariness fled me in a wash. "You what? My medicine?"

Wicked trotted into the library ahead of me, tail

held high as he cast his bright gaze on the wonder-land of stuff and places laid out before him.

Squeak!

My gaze shot to the enormous magical desk, finding the tiny, black-eyed critter trembling on its massive surface. *Oh no!*

"Wicked!" I screamed as his sparkling orange-gold gaze lifted toward the frightened sound.

Three things happened at once.

My medicine took off running, tail rigid behind him.

My new kitten hared off after him, a look of pure joy painting his adorable face.

And, I forgot I was tired, as I stumbled after the burgeoning disaster unfolding itself before my very eyes.

It was pretty much business as usual in the adventure that was my new life.

The End

READ MORE ENCHANTING INQUIRIES

If you enjoyed **Unbaked Croakies**, you might want to check out the rest of the series. Please enjoy Chapter One of **Tea & Croakies**, Book 2 of the *Enchanting Inquiries Paranormal Cozy Mysteries series* as my gift to you!

This is no boring librarian shushing people from behind a desk. This librarian corrals rogue magic. But more importantly, she has a frog and a cat, and she's not afraid to use them!

I knew when I woke up with a migraine that things were going to get interesting. As a magical artifact wrangler, it's not an unusual way to start my day. But I had no idea how bad it was going to get.

Until I found a frog sitting in my teacup.

Even that, I could explain to myself if I had to.

After all, I have a creative mind. But when the frog started talking to me, yeah, I was pretty sure I'd taken the wrong kind of pill that morning for my headache.

If only I'd realized then what I know now. The talking frog was just the beginning of my problems. And quite a beginning it was!

TEA & CROAKIES

⟩

Beware Pinching Chairs

I've been told from an early age that magic wrangling is a science. Color me skeptical. It's not that I don't believe it's a science. It's that, for me, the whole process is really more of a hit or miss, try until you die proposition. It's like I'm missing something that will make it easier. As if someone forgot to give me my magic wand when I reached my eighteenth birthday and came into my powers.

Or rather, my powers came into me. With a *crash, thump, grab your rump* kind of unexpectedness that left me hanging over the toilet horking and holding my head with both hands as it tried to split in two.

Even now, five years later, I still get the migraines. I wish I could say they've gotten easier over time. And maybe they have. But if you're making a comparison between a tsunami and a level 5 hurricane, it's really a distinction without a whole lot of difference for the people getting pounded by weather. Well, except one might kill you faster.

I'm thinking my shelf life might be a little bit longer these days, though I couldn't prove it.

At the moment, with a thousand tiny gnomes wearing spiked golf shoes and using pickle forks as walking sticks dancing on my brain, I was thinking it might be preferable to die faster anyway.

The world suddenly erupted in a series of explosions that had a familiar cadence to them. I hid under my long, brown hair and fought my lids to get them to open. But they fought back, eventually snapping closed again as the explosions stopped and the door my intruder had been banging on swung slowly open. "Naida? Are you awake?"

All evidence to the contrary, I was, unfortunately, awake. I grunted something even I couldn't decipher and my torturer took it as permission to come into my room.

"I closed up downstairs. Do you want me to make you some tea?"

My lips moved and more words nobody could understand eased through them. Fortunately, my loyal, if slightly annoying, assistant understood Migrainish Gibberish.

"I felt the magic arrive a few minutes ago, so I went ahead and closed up," she cheerfully said as she picked up my teapot and proceeded to bang out the Star-Spangled Banner with it on my stovetop.

Not really, of course. But only because she wasn't musically inclined and couldn't recreate the Star-Spangled Banner if her life depended on it.

"Ugh!" I said, hoping she could interpret that single non-word as "Please try to be quieter. My head is killing me."

Bang! "Oh say..." Crash "...can you see..." Clang "by the dawn's early light..."

"Sebille!"

She jerked to a halt as I sat bolt upright in my bed, my blue eyes flying open with outrage. I immediately regretted the decision to move, my brain pulsing unhappily inside my head and the soldiers with pickle forks breaking into a rowdy rendition of the Irish Chicken Dance. "You're killing me."

True to form, my non-serious friend simply rolled her almost iridescent green eyes. "Drama much?"

I put my head into my hands and groaned. "Why do I bother?"

A steaming mug appeared in front of my face. The sweet, floral scent undulated toward my nostrils in a siren song I could not resist. Taking the mug, I sniffed first, letting the sweet deliciousness infuse my sinuses.

The headache eased a bit just from that sniff,

and by the time I'd drained the mug a few minutes later, the pain was gone.

I sighed. "Are you sure you're not a witch? Tea never works this well when I make it."

Sebille dropped onto the edge of my bed. "You know I'm not a witch. I'm just tea-talented."

I would have sighed but the extra air rushing through my system probably would have enraged the soldiers with pickle forks. "Thank you. I was working up the courage to make myself some when you assaulted my door."

Sebille shook her head. "You always exaggerate so."

I glowered at her. "And you have zero compassion."

Shrugging, she tugged a strand of her bright red hair before tucking it behind a pointed ear. "That is unfortunately true."

No remorse. Which, BTW, perfectly matched her lack of compassion.

"Did you get a read on the wave?" I asked.

My assistant uncrossed a long, bony leg and tucked it underneath her, the other leg dangling over the edge of the bed. She wore her customary green and white striped socks and slightly pointed red shoes, making her look like the Wicked Witch of the West. Well, from the knees down, anyway. "No. But, I did get a sense it was important to Croakies."

Croakies was the name of my shop. Before you ask me why a magical artifact shop would be named Croakies, don't. I couldn't possibly tell you. That was the name of the store when I got the place from the previous Keeper of the Artifacts. She'd been kind of scattered, seeming more interested in moving onto her next great adventure than preparing me for mine. I hadn't gotten around to asking her where the name had come from. It had been all I could manage getting her to tell me how to flush the magical toilet in my apartment.

I mean, jiggling the handle as I sang, *Make me a Magic Muffin Mister*, wasn't just gross. It was also not at all intuitive.

I'm just sayin'.

Rather than trying to wrangle the information from the previous keeper, I silently promised myself that I'd change the name of the shop as soon as the paperwork was signed.

Best laid plans and all.

I'd tried to make the change. Multiple times. But the new sign I'd hung to replace the weather-worn wooden one bearing an ugly spotted frog and the name, *Croakies*, disappeared within hours and the old sign magically reappeared.

I'd tried burning the old sign once. It resurrected itself right back onto the front of my store.

I hadn't even been successful changing the name on paper. No matter how many times I filed a new name with the city. The old name simply reappeared on the paperwork in its place.

I gave up after the third try.

Croakies it was.

I had no idea why. But who was I to question the ways of the magical universe?

Sebille untangled her bony limbs and stood. "Do you want me to consult the mirror?"

I nodded. "Would you mind?"

She shrugged. "I'll be in the back room if you need me."

The "back room" of Croakies was the special area where all the magical artifacts lived. The front room was a bookstore. Though not your average bookstore. Even there, magic and supernormal reality dominated. But Croakies Books was available to everyone, which meant I got a lot of little old ladies looking for talking cat cozy mysteries and more than my share of ghost-busting wannabes.

As a city Sprite, Sebille made liberal use of the mirrors to gain access to magical news and happenings. Her family used streams and lakes and lived in toadstool houses. Sebille would disintegrate into a puddle of pique and rage if she had to live in a toadstool. That's why I'd dubbed her a city Sprite, though there really was no such thing. By contrast, her very large family found toadstool homes to be the height of comfort.

Part of my odd assistant's issue with the whole

"live in the woods in a toadstool" thing was that it required she maintain her traditional size of one and a half inches tall. Sebille had discovered she enjoyed being the size of the rest of the world, which enabled her to do all the stuff that was key to her existence. Such as drinking half-caff, mocha latte grande made with steamed almond milk and coconut sugar, and hanging out at the Vape bar with perfect strangers who told her everything about their lives and then wondered why they had.

Yeah, that was her other superpower.

Sebille lived in a one-room apartment over the vapery across the street. She said she loved the atmosphere of the place and had even created her own vape flavor with magical herbs. I'd tried it once when she was in the testing stage and I'm pretty sure I entered a separate dimension for twenty very long minutes.

That was the last time I was going to be vaping with Sebille.

"Let me just wash out this mug and I'll be right down," I told her as she started down the steps leading to Croakies' back room.

Sebille flicked a hand dismissively and disappeared down the steps with thunderous steps. I'd never understand how someone whose natural state was teeny tiny with iridescent purple and green wings could be so heavy-footed.

Then again, it could have something to do with

the pointy red shoes. They hadn't had her size in the shiny monstrosities and Sebille had been "absolutely certain" she couldn't go on with her life if she didn't get them. She'd bought them anyway and stuffed the toes with cotton balls.

Thus the clomping aspect to her descent down my stairs. I'd personally witnessed the shoes taking a flyer more than once. I'd even been nearly clocked on the head by one once.

Shaking my head, I moved into the kitchen and ran water into the mug, adding some soap to the mix. Then I rinsed it out and placed it upside down in the drainer on my counter.

My head still ached, but it was much better than it had been before the tea. I splashed cold water onto my face and squinted around for a towel, finally remembering I'd put it into the laundry the night before.

Reaching blindly for the paper towels, I encountered an empty roll.

In desperation, I tugged my shirt up and dragged it over my face, leaving a large wet spot on the bottom.

Whatever.

I headed down to the first floor, suddenly anxious to discover the source of my magical headache. The sooner we figured out which artifact needed rescuing, the sooner I could get pain-free.

The door leading to the bookstore was at the

bottom of the stairs. I stopped and peered through the glass, seeing an empty store and a *Closed* sign on the door. Just as Sebille had said.

I released breath I hadn't known I'd been holding. It had been a long day and, though I loved my job at the bookstore, I was relieved that my day job wouldn't be interfering with my night job for once.

I locked the interior door and turned toward the large, open room behind the stairs. As usual, the light in the place flickered over the artifacts, a rainbow of colors that shifted and shuddered, depending on which artifacts held sway at the moment.

There was a light switch I could use to disrupt the natural light of the artifacts, but I'd never used it. I'd never felt the need to disrupt the artifacts' natural energy. I liked that they lit the space around them with an energy all their own.

I found Sebille standing in front of an ancient, wood-framed standing mirror, hands on hips and shoulders stiff. I recognized the tiny figure who stared back at her from the age-marbled glass.

"Don't be such a derk!" Sebille's mother exclaimed in a voice amplified by magic. It was very strange to see the bug-sized woman's lips moving and to hear a voice as big as her full-sized daughter's. "You know we must do as the magic commands."

Sebille leaned closer, her frame rigid. I couldn't see her freckled face but I could picture it in my mind. In her rage, the Sprite's features would be sharp, her skin giving off an iridescent glow that changed color depending on how mad she was. I was relieved to see it was only a mild pink, which meant she was irritated, but she wasn't going to be tempted to send an atom-shattering blast of magic into the treasure mirror in her present mood.

"Sebille?" I said as I approached. I spoke more to distract her from getting any angrier than for any other reason. I gave her mother a smile and a finger wave. "Your Majesty."

The Sprite's wings fluttered with pleasure and her tiny form dipped on the air before surging back up to eye level in the mirror. "Hello, Naida. How is your headache?"

I wrapped an arm around Sebille. "Better, thanks to your daughter's superhero level tea making abilities."

The Sprite in the mirror smiled regally. "I am glad. I hope you can help him, Keeper. I really do. Now I have to go." She shot straight up, out of view. The pond in the background sparkled for a beat before beginning to waver and then disappeared behind a silvery cloud of nothingness.

"He?" I asked my assistant.

Sebille dropped angrily onto a chair, her expression murderous. "Don't ask." She yelped and shot straight into the air, grabbing her buttocks and turning to glare at the chair. The red velvet and gilded wood furniture shifted back and forth as if wagging its tail and then settled into inactivity again.

I was pretty sure the gilded arms sparkled for a moment before returning to normal. "Casanova's chair," I told her, a laugh burbling in my throat.

"I'm aware of that, Naida!" She snapped, rubbing her bottom and glaring at the chair. "We should put that thing in the closet."

I allowed my laugh to escape, shaking my head. "I have. Five times. It just keeps showing back up at the front of the shop."

She sighed. "Sometimes, I hate magical artifacts."

I gave her a wink. "Yeah, but magical artifacts luuurrrvvve you!"

She somehow missed the humor in my teasing. "In the questionable vernacular of my Sprite mother, don't be such a derk, Naida!"

Shaking my head, I pointed to the mirror. "Did your mother have any insights for us?"

"Nothing very useful. She said the magical wave was mixed and vague. All she got from it was that it concerned a man." She pinched bony shoulders toward her pointed ears. "Maybe one of the artifacts in the shop has gone rogue."

I glanced around at the seemingly jumbled mess of things which looked harmless and innocent but which definitely weren't either of those things. Nothing glowed or shimmied or just generally looked agitated. "If so, I'm not sensing it here. Are you?"

Sebille opened her mouth to reply but didn't get the chance.

From the back of the room came a loud thump. I hurried in that direction, Sebille hot on my heels. No further sounds occurred to help us pinpoint the problem. After hurrying down aisle after aisle of dusty objects that didn't seem to be out of place, we came to the end of the last aisle and found the source of the problem.

Actually, he was the source of many of my problems. But he was just so dang cute!

I jerked to a stop and cocked my head, glaring down into a pair of round, orange eyes.

"Mr. Wicked!" Sebille uttered in her most irritated tone. "What have you done?"

The cat narrowed its startling eyes, which were actually a really dark gold but they often looked orange in the low light. He skimmed a glance in my direction and gave me a long, broken "Meow," then looked down at the thick, dusty tome his bottom was resting upon.

"What are you doing in here, Mister?" I asked the gray kitten as I scooped him up and placed a kiss on top of his head. His purr rumbled against my chest as I snuggled him close.

Sebille bent down to pick up the ancient, leather-bound text the cat had apparently knocked to the ground. "This book is two hundred years old, Naida," she whined, her long fingers wrapping around the spine. "It's delicate..."

The book skimmed sideways, banging against my foot. I looked at Wicked and he seemed to smile, even as his gaze narrowed with innocence. "What are you up to, cat?"

He shoved his back paws into my belly and I released him, watching him drop gracefully to the ground. He twined around my legs a couple of times and then looked up, giving me another throaty "Meow!"

Sebille put hands on hips, expelling an angry sigh. "Blast you back to the hellish environs you came from, you wicked feli..."

I slammed a hand over her mouth. "Don't you dare!"

Sebille glared at me over my hand, and then slowly tugged my appendage from her face. "I'm going home."

My first instinct was to agree, but then I remembered the magic wave. "But we haven't found the magical artifact that needs protecting." Even to me, my voice sounded a bit whiny. I couldn't help it. Sebille and I were like oil and water, but without her help I was totally in the dark.

A truly frustrating experience which made me feel inadequate on a daily basis.

She tossed a hand over her shoulder and kept

walking. "You'll be fine. Let that damnable cat help you find it."

She slammed the door between the front room and the artifact library and I fought to keep from stamping my foot.

"Meow!"

I glanced down to find Mr. Wicked sitting beside the book, whacking it with one of his paws as if trying to kill a bug. "Here, young man. Don't destroy the magical items." I grabbed the thick book and lifted it, brushing grime from the floor off its leather cover.

To my horror, the cover seemed to roll underneath my fingers, as if basking in the rubbing action of my touch. I almost dropped it, barely keeping hold with the tips of two fingers as it finally stopped moving. "Ugh!" I shook my head at Wicked. He was watching me as if he expected me to do something interesting.

I opened the book and flipped through its gold-edged pages, noting the yellowed but surprisingly well-maintained condition.

The pages were entirely blank.

I frowned. "Why in the world?"

The front door slammed and I jumped, sighing. Setting the book back into its spot on the shelves, characterized by a rectangular, dust-free area midway up from the floor, I headed toward the front room. "Come on, Mr. Wicked. We need to close the shop. Miss Huffy left without locking the doors."

Wicked hung back for a moment. But, by the time I reached the door into the bookstore, he was bouncing along beside me, short gray tail stuck straight up behind him. The kitten loved the stacks of books inside my magical bookstore and he never missed an opportunity to explore beneath the rows of shelves and in the corners for scraps of paper, bits of fluff, or forgotten string.

Check out the entire series here: https://samcheever.com/books/#enchanting

ALSO BY SAM CHEEVER

If you enjoyed **Unbaked Croakies**, you might also enjoy these other fun mystery series by Sam. To find out more, visit the **BOOKS** page at www. samcheever.com:

Enchanting Inquiries Paranormal Mysteries - **For more fun adventures with Naida, Sebille, and Wicked!**
Reluctant Familiar Paranormal Mysteries
Yesterday's Paranormal Mysteries
Gainfully Employed Mysteries
Silver Hills Cozy Mysteries
Country Cousin Mysteries

ABOUT THE AUTHOR

USA Today and WSJ Bestselling Author Sam Cheever writes contemporary and paranormal mystery and suspense, creating stories that draw you in and keep you eagerly turning pages. Known for writing great characters, snappy dialogue, and unique and exhilarating stories, Sam is the award-winning author of 80+ books.

To learn more about Sam and her work, visit her at one of her online hotspots:
www.samcheever.com
samcheever@samcheever.com

www.ingramcontent.com/pod-product-compliance
Lightning Source LLC
Chambersburg PA
CBHW060532260626
47161CB00003B/870